TRANSFORMERS
BUMBLEBEE
The Junior Novel

TRANSFORMERS
BUMBLEBEE
The Junior Novel

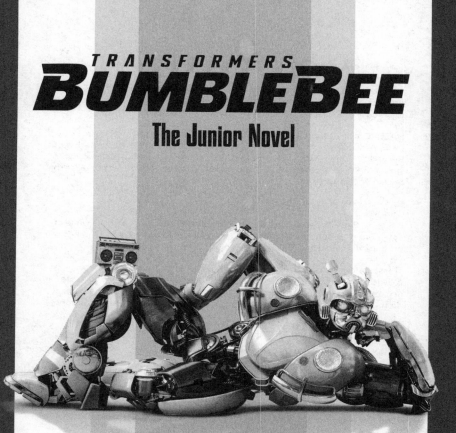

Adapted by Ryder Windham
Directed by Travis Knight
Produced by Don Murphy & Tom DeSanto,
Lorenzo di Bonaventura and Michael Bay

Little, Brown and Company
New York Boston

Cover design by Ching Chan.

Little, Brown and Company
Hachette Book Group
1290 Avenue of the Americas, New York, NY 10104
Visit us at LBYR.com

First Edition: November 2018

Little, Brown and Company is a division of Hachette Book Group, Inc.
The Little, Brown name and logo are trademarks of Hachette Book Group, Inc.

The publisher is not responsible for websites (or their content) that are not owned by the publisher.

Library of Congress Control Number 2018946189

ISBNs: 978-0-316-41919-2 (pbk.), 978-0-316-41917-8 (ebook)

Printed in the United States of America

LSC-C

10 9 8 7 6 5 4 3 2 1

Prologue

1982

Sparks sprayed out from robot B-127's damaged joints, and fluids poured from the wounds in his bulky, armored body as he stumbled through a cluster of trees. He'd been on the run for days, and he didn't have to consult his built-in health monitors to know he was close to complete power loss. His wounds were the result of his escape from a group of humans, members of a secret military organization, and also from a battle with another robot. The humans, including a man named Agent Burns, assumed that he was just a machine, and they seemed determined to destroy him. But he was much more than simply a machine.

B-127 was an Autobot—a peacekeeping soldier from the planet Cybertron, and an ally of Optimus Prime, the Autobots' towering leader. B-127 didn't know where Optimus Prime or the other Autobots were. The robot who had attacked him was a Decepticon, a sworn enemy of the Autobots, and it wouldn't be the only time they would come to Earth. They would keep coming until B-127 was captured. Both Autobots and Decepticons were capable of scanning Earth vehicles, then altering and rearranging their own bodies to assume the disguise of whatever vehicle they came across. But like all Autobots, B-127 needed precious green energy called Energon to help him change his form, and also to stay powered. He didn't have much Energon left.

B-127 gasped, producing a grinding noise in his upper chest. He had been wounded and left unable to speak. B-127 wondered how much farther he could walk.

He staggered past the trees and arrived at an empty campsite. He'd seen a sign for a town named Brighton Falls, but he wasn't sure where he was. He could hear people nearby, laughing and splashing in water. He tried to peer beyond the surrounding trees, and he thought he saw a lake. His vision blurred, and he collapsed, falling to his knees before landing hard against the ground. He could feel the last of his energy about to drain off when his automated survival system kicked in to shut down his remaining power.

He stopped hearing the swimmers, and then his vision began to fade. The last thing he saw was the swimmers' beat-up car parked at the edge of a dirt road.

The car was a yellow 1967 Volkswagen Beetle.

Agent Burns considered himself a man of action, someone who got results and got the job done, no matter how difficult. But he had failed in his task. B-127 was out there somewhere, still a potential threat.

As Burns sat in a secret bunker, brooding on the danger humanity had been in ever since those blasted Cybertronians had arrived, he started to plan. He would keep his home world safe. He would hunt down B-127 and, if necessary, destroy the robot before it could destroy Earth....

Chapter 1

1987

When her digital alarm clock's radio clicked on at eight AM on Saturday, the day before her eighteenth birthday, Charlie Watson was in no mood to wake up or get out of bed. And it didn't improve when the disc jockey predicted scorching heat for her hometown, Brighton Falls, California. Then the disc jockey started playing Madonna's latest hit single, "Who's That Girl."

"Shut up," Charlie muttered into her pillow. With her eyes still closed, she reached out and tried to hit the clock's snooze button. She missed three times before she knocked the clock off her night table. When the radio went silent, she hoped she'd broken it permanently.

She opened her eyes and climbed out of bed. She wore a T. rex T-shirt, boxers, and mismatched socks. Posters of David Bowie, Roxy Music, Adam Ant, and The Smiths decorated the walls of her messy bedroom. The only evidence of any effort to tidy up was a shoebox filled with her medals and trophies from her school's swim team. As she made her way to the bathroom, she brushed her fingers over a framed photo of herself, a few years younger, sitting with her father on the hood of a red 1959 Chevrolet Corvette. Her father had bought the Corvette as a restoration project, but it remained unfinished and still took up space in the two-car garage attached to Charlie's house.

After brushing her teeth and putting on some torn shorts and a shirt that she'd worn a few days earlier but hadn't bothered to wash, she grabbed the shoebox and went downstairs to the kitchen. Her mother, Sally, was washing dishes, and her stepfather, Ron, was drying. Sally was a nurse and was wearing scrubs. Sally and Ron giggled about something, and then they kissed. *Gross*, Charlie thought. She moved past them and dumped the shoebox and its contents into the garbage can.

Sally turned, looked at the garbage can, and said, "What are you—are those your diving trophies?"

Charlie shrugged. "They were taking up too much space in my room."

Sally lifted her gaze to meet Charlie's eyes. "You're gonna regret doing that someday. Just like you're gonna regret that mess you call your haircut."

Ignoring her mother, Charlie noticed the family dog, Conan, sniffing at the bottom of the garbage can. Then she noticed Conan's empty food bowl. "Did you guys feed Conan, or were you just gonna let him starve?"

"You're welcome to feed him yourself," Sally said, "and help out a little around here." She handed a bag of dog food to Charlie.

As Charlie poured food into the dog's bowl, she said, "You know how I could be an even bigger help? If I had a car, I could run errands, do stuff you don't want to do. Really contribute."

Sally sighed. "Charlie—"

"And whaddaya know," Charlie said, "it's my

birthday tomorrow. Perfect timing for a large cash gift. Five hundred bucks and I can finally finish the Corvette."

Sally sighed again. "Charlie, we've been over this. We're not in a position to throw gobs of money at a car we're not sure will ever even start. We just...We *can't*."

Before Charlie could protest, someone behind her said, "*Hiiiii*-yah!" She turned to see her twelve-year-old brother, Otis, enter the kitchen. He was wearing his martial arts uniform, a white *gi* with a yellow belt around the waist.

"Ah, Otis-san!" Ron said.

"*Hiiiii*-yah!" Otis said again. His hands launched out and chopped at the air in front of his stepfather.

Playing along, Ron fell back and said, "Oh no, he got me!"

Otis laughed. "Master Larry told me I'm the fastest one ever to get a yellow belt."

Sally beamed at Otis and said, "You look so grown up in that karate suit. My baby boy is becoming a man." Then she glanced at the kitchen clock and said, "Oh shoot. I'm gonna be late." She turned to Charlie. "Could you drop your brother at karate on your way to work?"

"I *could* if I had a *car*."

"Just let him follow you on your bike so nobody abducts him."

"Abducts him?" Charlie said. "You just said he's a grown man now."

Otis said, "If anyone tries anything, I'll rupture their spleen!" Next to the front door, Otis had propped up his skateboard. He grabbed it and said, "Come on, Charlie, let's go!"

Charlie groaned and followed Otis out of the house, which was at the end of a cul-de-sac that bordered a grassy marsh and had an ocean view from the backyard. They went to the driveway, where Charlie had parked her late-model moped. Despite her efforts to restore and tune the moped's engine, she couldn't get it to go faster than fifteen miles per hour. As she climbed onto the moped, Otis tied an old jump rope to the back of its frame. He tugged the rope to make sure it was secure and hopped onto his skateboard. Charlie started the ignition and took off at a crawl, pulling Otis along on his skateboard. Charlie kept her gaze forward, not looking at any of her neighbors' houses—if she was lucky, she could avoid eye contact with anyone. Towing her brother always made her beyond embarrassed.

Winding over back roads, they eventually arrived on Main Street, which was lined with trees, food markets, home-supply stores, restaurants, and other small businesses. They passed a woman sweeping the stoop outside her frozen-yogurt shop. She smiled and waved at them. Otis must have recognized her. He waved back with one hand as he held tight to the jump rope with the other. He smiled and said, "Morning, Mrs. Calloway. Beautiful weather this morning, isn't it?"

Mrs. Calloway nodded and laughed. As the moped *putt-putt*ed past her shop, Charlie glanced back at her brother and said, "You're such a suck-up, Otis."

"I'm *charming*," Otis said. "And I get a discount yogurt now. You should take notes."

Children wearing white *gi*s with cloth belts were on the sidewalk, waiting to enter Master Larry's karate dojo, which had Japanese words painted on its facade of large windows. As Charlie and Otis approached the dojo, Otis let go of the rope and angled for the sidewalk, where the other children saw him coming. He jumped and stomped on the tail end of the skateboard, flipping it into the air and catching it as he landed on the curb. Charlie heard Otis's friends laugh and cheer at his stunt as she rode on, dragging the jump rope along the street.

She arrived at Brighton Falls Boardwalk, an old amusement park with a wood-framed roller coaster and a stretch of arcade stalls and eateries that extended past a public beach. She worked at Hot Dog on a Stick, which was housed in a small shack that sold exactly what its name advertised. As she pulled up behind the shack, her boss, Craig, was opening up the shop. She knew Craig was twenty-two years old because he'd felt compelled to mention it at least three times that she could recall in the past week. Seeing Charlie, he tapped his watch and said, "You're seven minutes late."

"It's nine in the morning, Craig. I don't really

think there's a whole bunch of people craving wieners at this hour."

But just then, an impatient man bellied up to the hot dog kiosk and said, "Hello? *I've* been waiting!"

Craig shot a stern look at Charlie. Charlie exhaled as if she were letting out steam. She couldn't begin to imagine how managing a hot dog stand on the Boardwalk could give anyone such an incredible power trip.

She let Craig take care of the customer while she went into the shack and changed into her work uniform. As an employee and representative of Hot Dog on a Stick, she was required to wear a hideous multicolored shirt and hat with matching shorts. She didn't need a mirror to know she looked like a clown from a third-rate circus. And she didn't need a fortune-teller to know that her day probably wouldn't get any better.

Of course, then her day got much worse.

Chapter 2

It was almost noon, and Hot Dog on a Stick was bustling with hungry customers. Charlie scrambled behind the counter to keep up with orders as she churned a pump to make lemonade. She glanced at the customers and then, beyond them, saw a group of teenagers, mostly seniors from her high school, hanging out next to a parking lot, trying to look tough. Most of them wore acid-washed denim, tight pastel T-shirts, and flamboyant hairstyles that suggested they were also trying hard to look like a cast of extras for a pop-music video. At the center of the group was Tripp Summers, a tall, handsome boy with chiseled features and an easy smile. A cluster of girls that Charlie had aptly nicknamed the Pretty Mean Girls surrounded him. The prettiest—and meanest—of the bunch was the leader, Tina Lark, who drove a convertible BMW and never failed to mention that her family was loaded. Tina was eating a corn dog while she leaned in close to Tripp.

When Charlie was finally able to take a quick break, she spotted her friends Liz and Brenda, who worked at the corn dog stand, and waved them over. Liz and Brenda looked entranced as they stared at the Pretty Mean Girls. Liz said, "I gotta get some of those sock things. What do they call them? Leg warmers?"

Brenda nodded. "They look so cool on everyone."

"*So* cool," Liz said. "Who even thought of them?"

"A crazy person," Charlie said. She flicked her fingers and pointed from her upper thigh to her ankle. "If from here to here is the only part of you that's cold, something is wrong with you. It means you have a disease."

Liz and Brenda looked at each other. Liz cleared her throat, looked at Charlie, and said, "Oh, hey, um…We wanted to talk to you about something. We know your birthday's tomorrow."

"Yeah," Charlie said, "I was thinking we could just do something low-key. Get a burger. Count the days till we graduate. Are you cool to drive, Bren?"

Brenda looked at Liz and said, "Oh, uh..."

"What?" Charlie said. "What's wrong?"

Brenda looked at the ground. "No, it's just...I don't know if that's a good idea."

Charlie shifted her gaze from one girl to the other. "What do you mean?"

Brenda's face went red. She glanced at Liz for help. Facing Charlie, Liz said, "Look, we haven't known how to tell you this, but...You've just, like, changed a lot."

Charlie felt stunned and confused. "What?"

"You know..." Liz gestured with her fingers at Charlie. "The hair, the clothes. And you're just like..." Liz widened her eyes and frowned, trying to look depressed. "*All* the time."

Charlie leveled her gaze at Liz. "So what are you saying? You don't want to hang out with me 'cause I'm not whistlin' 'Dixie' every second?"

"No," Brenda said, "it's just, you haven't really been yourself since...you know."

"Since my dad died? No kidding, I haven't been myself."

Brenda sighed. "I'm sorry. We're really sorry."

Liz said, "We just don't feel like we're, like, a match anymore. It's not personal, it's just—"

Charlie was done listening. She grabbed a tray of food and brushed past Liz and Brenda so she could deliver the food to her customers, and she tried to concentrate on her job and ignore everything else. She knew that was the only way she could get through the next minute without bursting into tears.

As she carried the tray, a sixteen-year-old boy named Guillermo Gutierrez, also known as Memo, stepped away from the churro stand that was his place of employment for the summer. He tried to sound casual as he walked up to Charlie and said, "Hey, we've never met. I actually moved next door to y—"

"Sorry," Charlie snapped, "I can't. Sorry." She kept moving.

"Yep. Nope. Okay," Memo said as he turned around and walked back to the churro stand. When he returned, there was a police cruiser driving along the Boardwalk.

Sheriff Lock, a lean man with a strong jaw, was behind the wheel. He began to slow down as he approached the area where the high schoolers were gathered.

Seeing the sheriff, Tripp Summers said, "Let's get out of here." The teens started to move off, separating and drifting back to their cars in the parking lot. As Tripp turned quickly toward his red 1977 Camaro, he collided with Charlie, who was carrying the tray of hot dogs and lemonade.

Charlie never saw Tripp coming. Her tray and everything on it went flying. In an instant, lemonade, ketchup, mustard, and relish were splattered all over Tripp's T-shirt. Tripp looked down at his shirt, his mouth agape.

Charlie was mortified. "I'm so sorry," she said. She got down on her knees and scrambled to gather the fallen hot dogs, buns, and emptied cups back onto the tray.

Tina Lark and the rest of her Pretty Mean Girls gang moved in. Looking down at Charlie, Tina sang in a childlike voice, "Somebody's getting fired." Then she glanced at her friends, gestured to

Charlie's uniform, and said, "If I had to wear *that*, I would *pray* to be fired."

Charlie tried to ignore Tina. She looked at Tripp and said, "I'm really sorry."

Tripp grinned. "It's all right." He pulled off his soaked, messy shirt. A few of the Pretty Mean Girls sighed as they gazed at him. Tripp turned and started walking toward his car.

Tina deliberately bumped Charlie and said, "Oops," then she and the other girls followed Tripp to his Camaro. The girls jumped in with him, and they squealed when he started the engine.

Charlie watched the Camaro drive off. She carried the spoiled hot dogs and empty cups over to a trash bin and dumped them in. And then she went back to her job.

Later, when Craig handed her an envelope with a check in it, she looked at it with surprise. She'd forgotten it was payday. Maybe there was some way to salvage something out of the wreckage that had been her Saturday.

After work, and back in her street clothes, Charlie left the Boardwalk and rode her moped to Hank's Marine Repair and Parts, better known as Uncle Hank's, an establishment at the marina a few miles south of Main Street. On her way, she passed a recently built transmission tower, which was by far the tallest structure in Brighton Falls. The metal tower featured a mammoth dish antenna that dominated the skyline of the otherwise scenic marina. Many local citizens, including Uncle Hank, considered the tower among the ugliest structures on earth.

Uncle Hank's had started as a marina with a boating-supply store and repair shop, but Hank later developed the neighboring land so his operations included an automotive garage and an auto-salvage yard. Charlie left her moped outside the main building and found Hank seated behind the cashier's counter, holding his black-and-white Pocketvision television. Charlie guessed Hank was around seventy-five years old, but she allowed for the possibility that he was pushing a hundred. He ran his fingers through the remaining hairs on his head to make sure they covered at least a portion of his bald spot, then he tilted his small TV back and forth, angling its extendable aerial in different directions as he tried to tune in to a signal.

"Hey," Charlie said.

Without looking away from the Pocketvision's screen, Hank said, "Still working on your Corvette?"

Looking at his head, Charlie said, "Not as hard as you work on that comb-over." She reached into a pocket, pulled out her paycheck, and held it out so Hank could see she had $52.50 to spend. "Payday. What have you got for me?"

"Whatever you want," Hank said with a shrug. "Russians are gonna bomb us all to smithereens anyway."

Charlie nodded. "You're a fountain of positivity, Hank."

Taking a small crate with her, Charlie went outside. She worked her way past the boats in the marina and went to the higher ground, where upside-down fishing boats and broken-down cars rested in the salvage yard. She started looking for parts that she could use for the restoration of her Corvette. She'd found a few odds and ends, and placed them in her crate, when she climbed up onto an old speedboat that rested on a metal stand. She started poking around the boat's belly and soon found and removed an ignition coil. She tossed it into the crate with the other parts, then jumped off the boat.

Her jump caused the speedboat to rock on its stand and knock the boat next to it, and then that boat knocked another, which slipped off its stand. Startled, Charlie turned in time to see the third boat as it slipped. She also saw it snag and pull a moldy tarpaulin from a vehicle resting beside it. She could see only a small part of the vehicle, a yellow metal fender.

She walked over to the partially covered vehicle and peeled back the tarp. She found a yellow Volkswagen Beetle, rusted and covered with cobwebs.

"Hello," Charlie said to the derelict Beetle. "Where'd you come from, and what can you do for me?" She knew that Volkswagens had rear-mounted engines and that the curved hood concealed a luggage compartment. Curious, she tried to open the hood, but it wouldn't budge. Then she tried the driver's door and managed to pull it open. As she climbed in, she didn't notice a small hive of bees nesting in the wheel well. She also didn't notice an unusual insignia in the middle of the steering wheel, an insignia that didn't look anything like Volkswagen's *VW* logo.

Inside, the seat covers were frayed and smelled of mildew. Charlie was surprised to find a key in the ignition. She turned the key and was even more surprised when the engine sputtered to life and the radio kicked on. The engine noise lasted a full second before it died, but the radio stayed on, spewing white noise, loud crackling and hissing sounds.

"No way," Charlie said. She knew Uncle Hank routinely removed batteries from cars before placing them in the salvage yard, so finding one with a working battery seemed like a minor miracle. She rotated the radio's tuning knob back and forth, searching for a station, but all she could hear was more white noise.

Charlie was still rotating the tuning knob when

she heard buzzing that had nothing to do with the radio. Several bees from the wheel well had drifted into the car. Charlie said, "Whoa!" She switched off the radio, launched herself out of the Beetle, and slammed the door behind her.

She grabbed and carried her crate of scavenged parts back to Hank's shop. After dumping the crate's contents onto the counter, she said, "I'll give you thirty bucks for all of it."

Hank glanced at the ignition coil that Charlie had taken from the speedboat. "I could get twice that for the coil alone."

"Yeah, but you won't," Charlie said.

Hank shrugged.

"Thanks, Hank," Charlie said. "Hey, where'd you get that Beetle?"

But Hank wasn't listening. He was still fiddling with his Pocketvision TV and its aerial. "Nuts," he said. "Ever since they put up that ugly transmission tower, I can't get a signal to watch my news."

Charlie placed thirty dollars from her wallet on the counter and walked out, carrying the crate of parts to her moped. She secured the crate and took off, leaving the marina. As she rode past the transmission tower, she thought about how much Uncle Hank loathed it. He was right, she decided. The tower really was an eyesore.

As she rode home, her thoughts drifted to Liz and Brenda, and she felt sad and angry all over again. She tried to push them out of her mind. She tried to think about the parts that she'd just bought and started planning how she would use them for her Corvette. She wished she could start the Corvette's engine as easily as she'd started the old Beetle's, but because the Corvette's engine was still missing so many pieces, she knew that wouldn't happen anytime soon.

But she also knew that the sooner she had a car, a *working* car, the sooner she could leave Brighton Falls. She wasn't sure where she'd go, but she was tired of feeling stuck and wished she were gone already.

She arrived at the cul-de-sac, left her moped in the driveway, and carried her crate into the garage. The garage had a worktable and numerous tools, including a bench grinder and a mechanic's creeper for working beneath cars. It was also equipped with an old television and a VCR, which were on a small cart with wheels. The walls were lined with shelves that held everything from a stereo system to camping gear.

The Corvette rested where it had been for the past several years. Charlie had convinced herself that she was eager to begin working on the Corvette, even on the night before her eighteenth birthday, but when she saw its incomplete engine on the industrial dolly and other parts laid out on the floor and on her workbench, she just sighed.

She knew she was in for a long night.

"You have got to be kidding me," Charlie said, talking to the Corvette.

She was lying on the creeper, her legs sticking out from under the car. Her new acquisitions from Uncle Hank's were spread out across a tarp on the floor beside her. "Of course you need a new valve, too," Charlie muttered. "You need a new *everything*."

She groaned. Holding a grease rag, she slid out from under the car. She looked at all the parts she'd placed on the tarp, then at various parts within reach. She felt overwhelmed and defeated.

"This is never gonna happen," she said. She looked up at the ceiling. She thought of her father. "I can't do it, okay? I give up. It's never gonna happen."

She threw the grease rag aside and rose from the floor. She went through the door that connected the garage with the house's kitchen. The house had an open floor plan, and from the kitchen area, Charlie had a clear view into the living room. She saw her mother, stepfather, and brother on the sofa, laughing as they watched TV. She didn't know what they were watching or why they were laughing so hard, and she wasn't curious to find out. She just didn't care.

Without a word, she went upstairs to her bedroom and got into her pajamas. She glanced at the photo of herself with her father before she set the timer on her digital alarm clock, switched off the light on her night table, and crawled into bed. She didn't have high expectations for her birthday, but maybe her family might try to surprise her. If that fell through, she'd have to find her own birthday plans, now that she knew she definitely wasn't going to celebrate with Liz and Brenda.

Things could be worse, she thought. *You could be alone and completely forgotten, like that Beetle at Uncle Hank's junkyard.*

She wondered how the yellow Beetle wound up at Uncle Hank's. She was still thinking about it when she fell asleep, and when she began dreaming about driving to faraway places.

Chapter 3

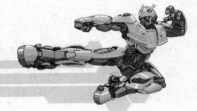

On Sunday morning, when the radio of Charlie's alarm clock clicked on to blast "Manic Monday" by the Bangles, Charlie was lying facedown on top of her covers. Without opening her eyes, she reached out and knocked the alarm clock off the night table.

She dragged herself out of bed, stumbled to a stop before a mirror, and studied her reflection. Her face looked puffy, her pajamas were rumpled, and her hair was a disaster. "Happy eighteenth," she said without a trace of enthusiasm.

Still in her pajamas, she trudged down to the kitchen. Sally was wearing scrubs, and Ron was getting ready to head off to work. Charlie said, "Hey."

"Good morning, birthday girl," Sally said. "You look...nice."

Charlie offered no response. She knew that she looked like a disaster.

Sally said, "How does it feel, huh? You're an official adult today! I miss eighteen. I had these boots that came up to here." She patted her legs about two inches above her knees. "I was one hundred pounds soaking wet, toolin' around town with my friends all night." She turned to Ron. "What were you like at eighteen?"

"Oh, you know," Ron said, "motorcycle, long hair that went on for days. You wouldn't have liked me."

Sally giggled, then picked up a box from the counter and handed it to Charlie. "Quick, open your gift, honey. I'm late for work."

"Thanks," Charlie said, taking the box. She opened it and pulled out a bike helmet. The helmet was pink with daffodils painted on it. She wondered if the helmet was a gag gift, and if it might conceal another present, like an envelope with a check in it. She turned the helmet over in her hands so she could see every side of it, including the inside, but she found herself disappointed. She stared at the helmet, knowing she should say *something*. "A helmet," she said. "With daffodils painted on it."

Sally nodded. "Ron and I keep reading the news

about people on mopeds getting run down and having head injuries. You need to wear that from now on! I don't care if it's not the law, it's *our* law. Oh, and I need you to be in charge of your brother today, too, okay? I know it's your birthday, but…I need you to."

Charlie looked at her mother. "I can't think of *anything* that would bring me more joy."

"Well, good, then," Sally said, clearly sensing Charlie's sarcasm, "because we're out of other options."

Ron grinned. "I actually have a little gift for you, too, Charlie. It's small, but from the heart." He handed her a wrapped package.

Charlie tore off the wrapping paper to find a book. She looked at the front cover. The title was *SMILE FOR A CHANGE: The Benefits of a Positive Attitude!* She didn't know what to say. She looked at Ron.

"A smile is a powerful thing," Ron said, as if he had imparted incredibly serious information. "It releases endorphins, it makes you feel more positive, it says to the world, 'I'm fun and approachable!' There's a whole chapter about how people who smile more often actually have more friends."

"Really," Charlie said.

"Yeah! They've studied it." Ron tapped the book's cover. "Wonderful book. I saw it and said, *That's for Charlie.* I think it's gonna change your whole outlook." Ron's mouth twisted into a broad, happy smile that showed off all his teeth.

Sally smiled, too. Charlie didn't. Ron and Sally were still smiling as they walked out of the house.

Charlie left the gifts in the kitchen and returned to her bedroom. She flopped down onto her bed and squeezed her eyes shut. She hated everything. She wanted to feel better but didn't know how or where to begin.

She sat up and opened her eyes, and her gaze happened to fall on a picture she'd taped to the wall. The picture was a few years old, and it showed her laughing with Brenda and Liz. She pulled the picture down, crumpled it up, and tossed it into the wastebasket.

She got out of bed and looked at the giant 1987 Chevrolet calendar hanging on the wall. She counted off the months until the following June, when—if all went according to plan—she would graduate from high school. "Ten more months," she said, and winced. She didn't want to be stuck in Brighton Falls for another second.

She felt light-headed and weighted down at the same time. She sat on the edge of her bed. She looked at her alarm clock, which was still on the floor where she'd batted it, its cord still plugged into the nearby wall socket. She stared at the clock, waiting for the minute to change. It couldn't change fast enough.

Ten more months.

"No," she said, standing up fast. "*Today.* You have to take charge of your life *today.*"

She paced back and forth, thinking. *What should I do? What* can *I do? What can I do* right now?!

She looked around her room, and her eyes locked onto the photo of her with her father and the Corvette. And as she looked at the photo, an idea came to her. An idea that she didn't have to think about twice. She knew it was a good idea, maybe the best she'd ever had.

There was just one problem: Otis.

Her brother wasn't in his bedroom. She ran downstairs and looked for him in the living room and kitchen. She found Conan sleeping on the rug in front of the TV, but no sign of Otis. She heard a loud *whack* from outside. She ran out the front door and found Otis standing beside his skateboard as he placed a plank of wood up against a parked car's front bumper to create a makeshift ramp.

Charlie walked over to Otis, grabbed him by his shirt collar, and pulled him close to her. "I'll be right back," she said. "If you die while I'm gone, I will kill you, Otis. Do you hear me?"

"Ew," Otis said, squirming in Charlie's grip. "Let go of me!"

Charlie let him free with a smirk, and he stumbled backward. He glowered at her and said, "You're lucky I didn't pull a karate move and break your fingers off!"

Charlie went over to her moped, climbed onto it, and took off at fifteen miles per hour, leaving Otis and the cul-de-sac behind.

"I want the Beetle," Charlie said.

Seated at his desk in his supply shop's office, Uncle Hank was baffled by Charlie's statement. He said, "What?"

"The yellow Beetle," Charlie said. "I want it. I'll make you a deal. If I get it started, it's mine."

Hank thought about it for two whole seconds. "That doesn't sound like a deal. That sounds like you just taking my car."

"If I get it started, I keep it and work here every day for a year. I'll scrub the grease stains off your floors."

Hank kept his gaze on Charlie but cocked his head to the side. Charlie didn't know whether he was considering her offer or thought she was crazy. She gestured to the file cabinets behind his desk and said, "I'll organize every scrap of paper in this office. I'll even detail your horrible, disgusting toilets."

Hank remained silent as he continued staring at Charlie.

"It's my birthday," Charlie said. *"Please."*

Hank could see the desperation in Charlie's eyes. He shook his head. "Sorry. No deal."

Charlie blinked and pursed her lips. "But...why?"

"'Cause we ain't hiring. It's yours, kid."

Charlie's eyes went wide. "Thank you! Thank you! Thank you!" She turned and ran for the door.

"And my toilets are gorgeous!" Hank shouted after her, but she was already through the door and running for the salvage yard.

The Beetle was where she'd left it, under a tarpaulin at the end of a row of upside-down boats. She pulled off the tarp and looked at the Beetle. Even though it was covered with muck and patches of rust, she smiled as she inspected it. She couldn't believe it was hers.

She moved to the back of the car and popped the engine compartment. Sludge had caked over much of the air-cooled, four-cylinder engine. She got a rag and a brush to remove the sludge, then she borrowed some spare tools and solvents from Uncle Hank so she could work on the engine's parts.

Morning turned to late afternoon, and she was still tinkering with the engine. Her hands and face were smudged with grease when she finally worked up the nerve to get behind the wheel and test the ignition. She said, "Please please please…"

She turned the key.

Nothing.

And then the engine sputtered to life.

"Oh yes!" Charlie shouted. "Yes!" She patted the steering wheel. "I love you!"

She was so happy and excited that she kissed the steering wheel and got a mouthful of dust. But the engine continued to purr.

Several minutes later, she drove the Beetle out of the scrapyard. As she went past the windows of Uncle Hank's shop, she honked the horn and waved. Hank smiled and waved back at her.

Even though the Beetle's engine still made weird sputtering noises, Charlie grinned as she drove it all the way home. She'd have to get her moped later, but it was worth it. She was parking the car in front of the garage when Otis came out of the house. He was eating a popsicle and had a small plastic bandage on his elbow.

Otis looked at the Beetle, and his face scrunched up with disgust. "What are you doing with that hunk of junk?"

"Don't worry about it, Otis," Charlie said as she got out of the car.

"You were gone for five hours," Otis said. He held up his arm and displayed his bandage. "My elbow bled. If you think I'm not telling Mom on you, you're dead wrong."

Charlie placed her hands on her hips and glared at her brother. "Otis, how about you try being a decent human being for once in your life, and just say, 'Happy birthday, Charlie.'"

Otis shifted his gaze to the ground and shuffled his feet. Charlie guessed he felt guilty. "Get the hose," she said. "You're gonna help me wash it."

Otis snorted. "No, I'm not."

So much for guilt, Charlie thought, but she knew how to handle her brother. She said, "Do you want rides to places, or not?"

Otis raised his eyebrows, and Charlie knew she had him.

They gathered cleaning supplies from the garage, and Charlie put Otis to work. They brushed off the dust, dirt, and cobwebs from the Beetle's exterior before Charlie used a long stick to remove the now-abandoned beehive from the wheel well. They buffed the rust off the fenders, and Charlie coaxed out a dent on the passenger door. She tried again to open the Beetle's hood, but it remained stuck in place.

Otis helped Charlie wash the car with soap and water before he wandered into the garage to play a video game on the garage's television. As Charlie carried a bucket of filthy suds to the drain in the driveway, the Beetle began to roll, moving slowly after her. Charlie heard a squeaking noise, turned to see the Beetle inching toward her, and thought, *This car must want to keep me close.* She laughed as she stepped around to the driver's side of the car, reached in, and jammed on the hand brake. No need to let her dream roll away on the very first day.

She used her mother's cordless vacuum to clean the Beetle's filthy interior. When she was done, the sun was beginning to set. The Beetle's yellow exterior looked much cleaner and brighter, and Charlie was exhausted. She took a few steps back to admire the car and said, "It looks amazing."

Otis looked away from his video game, saw Charlie standing beside the Beetle, and said, "It still looks like something a homeless hippie lives out of."

Charlie smirked. It didn't matter. She was already thinking about all the places she'd drive. Charlie Watson had a *car*.

Chapter 4

Charlie felt very proud as she drove the Beetle down Main Street in Brighton Falls. Otis looked less enthusiastic as he sat in the front passenger seat. Clearly, he was hoping none of his friends would see him riding in such a junky car.

"You're too young and dumb to understand this now," Charlie said, "but a car means freedom. Independence. A car changes everything."

Otis rolled his eyes. He started to ask Charlie about a suspicious-looking hole in the upholstery— a bullet hole? But before he could get a word out, the Beetle made a coughing noise and released a dark puff of smoke from its tailpipe. The noise made Otis jump in his seat.

Charlie turned on the Beetle's radio and tried to tune in several stations, but all she got was screeching static. She switched off the radio and wondered if she could get a cheap replacement at Uncle Hank's. The Beetle made grinding, rumbling noises as she brought it to a stop at a red light.

"What's that racket?" Otis said. Other motorists were staring at the Beetle. "Oh no. Everyone is looking at us!" Looking even more embarrassed, he slid down low in the seat.

The light turned green, and Charlie started driving forward. The Beetle traveled only a few feet before it made a sad, choking noise, and then the engine stalled, bringing the Beetle to a dead stop in the middle of the intersection. The driver behind Charlie leaned into his horn.

"Chill out!" Charlie said. She restarted the Beetle. It lurched two more feet into the intersection and stalled again. More cars started honking. "Oh, come on, come on!"

Tina Lark, driving her convertible, pulled around the Beetle and glanced at it with disgust. The honking continued. Someone shouted, "Learn to drive, loser!"

Charlie turned the key again and waited. The Beetle sputtered. Otis turned to face her and said, "Happy birthday, Charlie." Then he got out of the car, slammed the door, and started walking back to their house.

Night had fallen by the time Charlie managed to get the Beetle back home and into the garage. She hit the steering wheel. "You stupid car!" She got out, slammed the door, and felt her frustration turn into rage. Without thinking, she kicked the front bumper. The front right section of the car fell against the garage floor with a loud *clank*.

"Oh great," Charlie said. She knelt to inspect the damage. She was surprised to see that the section that had fallen was still partially attached to the car. Then she noticed that the damaged piece resembled a mechanical arm.

She looked closer and saw things that shouldn't have been on the car: strange joints and cogs that were definitely not original parts. She said, "What the heck?"

She traced one joint back to where it disappeared under the hood, which still wouldn't open. Hoping to see more of the joint, she lay down on the creeper and pushed herself under the Beetle. She couldn't find anything unusual. She examined the drive shaft and shock absorbers. Everything looked normal.

Then she noticed something strange. Two blue lights, inches above her, began to radiate. The Beetle's front axle snapped in two, spun, and locked into the muffler with a *thunk*. And then all across the undercarriage, parts began moving, snapping, and reconnecting.

Charlie's eyes went wide, and her body froze against the creeper. She was afraid to budge as the chassis and molding peeled back and started to reorganize their forms, like shape-shifting building blocks. And then the car began to rise, pushing itself up from the floor. As the last parts clunked into place, Charlie realized that the Beetle was no longer a car at all.

It was a twelve-foot-tall, giant yellow robot.

The robot was stooped over to keep his head and shoulders from scraping against the garage's ceiling. His head held two electric-blue eyes, and both gazed straight at Charlie.

Charlie's mouth fell open, but she was too frightened to scream. Keeping her eyes locked on the robot, she rolled off her creeper and scrambled to her feet. She backed away until she hit the door that led into the house. As she fumbled for the doorknob, she watched the robot retreat from her and bump into the far wall. An old kite had been resting on a high shelf, but at the robot's impact, the kite fell from the shelf and fluttered down onto his head.

The kite's string also fell around the robot. The robot turned his head as he raised his metal hands, and the movement tangled the string around his neck and fingers. As he struggled with the string, Charlie thought the robot looked concerned and anxious, and also less menacing.

Still hunched over in the cramped garage, the robot freed himself from the kite and string and placed the kite back on the shelf. The robot looked again at Charlie, and something about his eyes made Charlie certain that he wasn't a threat. She realized he was terrified.

Taking a deep breath, she stepped away from

the door and looked closer at the robot's body. She recognized the Beetle's headlights and grille and other VW parts that she had washed with care just a few hours earlier. She didn't know how her Beetle had changed into a robot, but she had no doubt that the robot was somehow also her car and her responsibility.

A loud knocking came from the door behind Charlie. And then she heard her mother from the other side. "Charlie? What was that noise?"

"Nothing!" Charlie said. "I'm fine, I—" She turned around and saw the doorknob turn. She leaped toward the door, hoping to stop it from opening, but she wasn't fast enough. As her mother peered into the garage, Charlie tried to block her view. "Everything's cool, Mom. Go back to bed."

But Sally gazed past Charlie and said, "What the heck is that?"

Charlie squeezed her eyes shut, not knowing what to say. Then her mother said, "What's that car doing in our garage?"

Charlie opened her eyes and turned around. The robot was no longer in sight, but in his place was the old yellow Beetle, resting on its tires beside the Corvette. Charlie breathed a sigh of relief. "Oh," she said. "Yeah, that car. It's mine. Uncle Hank gave it to me."

Surprised, Sally said, "What? When?"

"Today. It actually runs."

Sally frowned. "It looks like it was pulled out of a swamp."

"Okay, Mom," Charlie said, sounding stung, as if she didn't want her car to hear such negative comments. "It's sitting right *there*."

"I wish you would've told me before you just brought it home."

"Anyway," Charlie said, "I'm in the middle of some stuff, so…" She gestured for her mother to leave.

"All right, fine," Sally said. "I'll get out of your hair. But tell me things next time. I'm your mother." She left the garage and closed the door behind her.

Charlie waited, listening to her mother's footsteps. When she was sure her mother had gone back to bed, she approached the Beetle again. Keeping her voice low, she said, "You still…in there?"

The Beetle did not respond in any way.

Nervous, Charlie reached out and brushed her fingers across the side of the car. The Beetle's right fender fell again and hit the floor with another loud clank. The noise made Charlie flinch away from the car. "Okay, all right," she said. "Little jumpy, sorry."

She bent down to study the broken piece and realized that it was indeed one of the robot's arms. Moving with care, she reached out and tightened a loose joint where the arm connected with the car. She was still twisting at the joint when the car started to rearrange its shape again, shifting back into robot form.

Charlie held her breath and tried not to freak out. As the robot stood up, a piece of one shin flopped down and clanged against the floor. The robot reached down and tried to put the piece back on, but it wouldn't stay. The robot tried four more times before he swung hard at his own shin, banging the piece into place. He left a dent in the metal, but the piece held.

"That's *one* way to do it," Charlie said. She took a step back from the robot so she had a better view of him. "Hi."

The robot emitted a low buzzing noise.

"Are you...do you speak?"

The robot opened his mouth and tried to answer but produced only broken electronic noises. He shook his head and tried again but failed. He moved his metal fingers up to his neck and touched his damaged throat. A whirring noise that sounded almost like a whimper came from the side of his neck. He looked at Charlie and backed away from her.

"I won't hurt you," Charlie said. She trembled as she moved closer. She reached out to touch one of his arms and hoped that he would understand she wanted to help.

The robot looked at Charlie's hand, which was tiny compared with his own. He lowered his head until his metal cheek pressed against her hand. Charlie looked at the robot's wide face. She blinked. He blinked in response.

Charlie whispered, "Can you understand me?"

The robot nodded.

"What are you?"

The robot looked at the ceiling.

"Where did you come from?"

The robot shook his head. Charlie wondered how much, if anything, the robot knew about his past or about his own identity. She said, "It's okay; we'll take it slow."

The robot extended one of his big metal fingers to gently tap Charlie's chest. Charlie was wearing a T-shirt with a logo from one of her favorite bands. She looked down at it and said, "You like my shirt? You're a heavy metal fan?"

The robot shook his head. He tapped her chest again, then cocked his head, and Charlie guessed he was trying to ask a question.

"Me?" she said. "You want to know who I am?"

The robot nodded.

"My name is Charlie. Charlie Watson. I'm eighteen. Today, actually." She smiled. "What's your name?"

The robot shook his head again.

"You don't have a name, or you're not sure?"

The robot emitted a pitiful buzzing noise.

"Aw, you sound like a sad bumblebee," Charlie

said. "How about I call you that for now? *Bumble-bee.* Goes with your outfit, too." She gestured to the robot's yellow-and-black form.

The robot shrugged.

Charlie glanced at a clock and realized she couldn't stay in the garage all night without making her mom suspicious. Her mom would *definitely* want to check in on her and would notice if she wasn't in her room.

Bumblebee saw Charlie start for the door and shifted his body parts until he once again looked like an old, dinged-up Beetle.

Great, Charlie thought.

Charlie left the garage and went to her messy bedroom. She was almost asleep when it occurred to her that she still knew practically nothing about Bumblebee, including where he'd come from or how he'd wound up at Uncle Hank's salvage yard. As she drifted into sleep, she had the distinct impression she should keep Bumblebee's "ability" a secret. No one else could know that he was anything other than an old Volkswagen Beetle.

No one.

Miles away, two Cybertronians argued in the desert. Named Shatter and Dropkick, they were on a mission to hunt down the annoyingly hidden B-127. Sent to this backwater planet by their leader, they knew B-127 was somewhere in the area. If only the coward would show his face, they could capture him and be done with it. And then the fun would begin....

Chapter 5

Charlie was so eager to see Bumblebee that she woke up before her alarm clock went off. She pulled on her bathrobe, grabbed her toothbrush, and squeezed a dollop of toothpaste onto it. She brushed her teeth as she ran down the stairs to the kitchen. She bounded past Otis, who was pouring himself a large bowl of cereal, and Ron, who was on his way out the front door. "Mornin'," Charlie said as she yanked the toothbrush out of her mouth. "See you later."

Ron said, "Where are you off to so fast?"

"Nowhere. Have a nice day!" She spat toothpaste into the sink and smiled at Ron and Otis before she sprinted for the door to the garage.

Otis said, "What's wrong with her?"

Obviously believing his present to Charlie must have had a very positive effect on her, Ron smiled and said, "Sometimes, all you need is the right advice." He held his head high as he left the house.

Still carrying her toothbrush, Charlie entered the garage and said, "Mornin', Bumblebee. How do you—?"

Charlie froze. Bumblebee wasn't in the garage.

"Bee? Where are you?" Charlie walked in a circle, searching the garage's walls, shelves, and storage bins for any sign of the shape-shifting Beetle. She found nothing. Her toothbrush fell from her hand. She started to panic.

She ran out of the garage and into the front yard. She'd hoped to find Bumblebee parked on the street, but he wasn't there, either. Looking up the street, she saw Ron driving away in the station wagon.

"Oh, Bumblebee," Charlie muttered, "where did you go?" She was so preoccupied with her search that she didn't notice a dark-haired boy emerge from the house next door. The boy was Memo, who still had yet to successfully introduce himself to Charlie. He was holding a superhero comic, but when he saw Charlie, he tossed the comic into a nearby bush so she wouldn't think he was a nerd.

Charlie ran back into her house. Frantic, she entered the kitchen, saw her brother eating his cereal, and said, "Otis, have you seen my car?"

"Unfortunately, yes," Otis said between mouthfuls, "and my eyes are still scarred."

Charlie resisted the urge to scream. "Have you seen my car *today*?!" She gestured to the door to the garage. "It's gone. Someone stole it."

"No, idiot," Otis said. "Mom took it. She had to take Conan to the vet. He ate a rubber glove or something, and Ron needed the station wagon."

Realizing that no one had stolen Bumblebee, Charlie exhaled with relief and said, "Oh, thank goodness." But then she considered what Otis had said about their mom taking the car, and she said, "Wait."

And then she realized waiting was a bad idea.

With her bathrobe flapping at her legs, Charlie ran out of the house again and jumped onto her moped. Memo walked over to her and said, "Hello, me again, we never officially met. We just moved in, and I wanted to—"

"Sorry! Can't right now."

"Nope. Yep. Okay."

Memo sadly watched Charlie speed off on her moped.

Seated behind the wheel of the yellow Beetle, Sally Watson drove through a Brighton Falls neighborhood, trying to soothe Conan, who groaned as he lay on the back seat.

"I know, buddy," Sally said. "Hang in there. You can't eat everything you see. This is a good life lesson for you."

If Sally had glanced in her rearview mirror, she might have seen Charlie on her moped, racing to catch up with Bumblebee. But Bumblebee somehow spotted Charlie traveling behind him, and he extended his robot arm to wave at her.

Conan looked out the window and started barking.

Approaching an intersection, Sally began to slow down, and Charlie was able to pull up beside the Beetle. Sally looked out her window. Seeing

Charlie on the moped, Sally jerked back against her seat and said, "What are you doing, Charlie?"

"Mom, you have to pull over!"

Sally noticed that Charlie was wearing a bathrobe. "What's going on?"

While Charlie seemed to struggle for a good answer, she pointed to the curb and said, "Park there."

After Sally pulled over to the curb, Charlie got off her moped and leaned on her car. She whispered just loud enough so Sally couldn't make out her saying, "Stop it. Put your robot stuff away."

Charlie pushed her moped up onto the grass beside the curb. As Charlie walked back to the driver's side of the car, Sally said, "You gave me a heart attack. I thought I was being carjacked! I'm taking Conan to the vet."

"I know," Charlie said. "Otis told me. And I…I want to go with you."

"What?"

Charlie looked to the back seat. "I…I'm worried about Conan. He's my dog, too." She looked back at her mother. "I should be there!"

Sally pursed her lips. "You really *want* to go to the vet with me?"

"What, I can't love my dog? Sue me for having a big heart. Get out; I'll drive."

"Charlie—"

Charlie opened the driver's door and gestured for her mother to move. Flustered, Sally got out of the car. She went around it and got into the front passenger seat while Charlie settled in behind the wheel. Sally said, "You weren't wearing your helmet, by the way."

After the vet took care of Conan and patched him up, Charlie drove Sally and Conan back home. Charlie kept the Beetle's engine running while Sally carried Conan into the house. "Love you, Conan!" Charlie said as she blew a kiss to the dog.

Sally looked at Charlie. Charlie knew her mother was suspicious—Charlie had never been overly fond of Conan before. Charlie waited for Sally to shut the front door, then said, "All right, Bee, we need to go over a few things."

The Beetle responded with a clanking noise, and then they drove off. They traveled to the outskirts of Brighton Falls and then onto a series of back roads. They turned onto a dirt lane bordered by tall trees with sunlight shafting down through the leaves. Charlie thought Bumblebee's engine sounded better, almost as if it were producing happy noises.

They arrived at a secluded beach cove and came to a stop. Large rocks bordered the sandy parking area. Charlie got out of the Beetle, walked across the sand, and looked around to make sure that she and Bumblebee were alone. Turning back to the car, she said, "Okay, all clear."

Bumblebee changed so rapidly from a car into a robot that he accidentally kicked up sand, which showered down on Charlie. Charlie's mouth fell open with surprise, and she immediately regretted it. As she spat out sand and began brushing more sand off her head and shoulders, she said, "I'm rethinking the beach."

Seeing that Charlie's hair was still covered with sand, and looking eager to help, Bumblebee reached out to push his large metal fingertips through her hair. Unfortunately, he only managed to tangle her hair more.

Charlie tried to block his fingers and said, "I'm good, I'm good."

Ever helpful, Bumblebee wrapped one hand around Charlie and picked her up, lifting her off the ground so he could try shaking the sand off her. Charlie gasped and said, "This is really becoming overkill."

Bumblebee put her back down. As Charlie brushed off the remaining sand, she said, "Look, this is serious, Bee. Humans aren't cool about things they don't understand. If they find you, they'll probably lock you up in a lab and cut you into little pieces. The only person you can show yourself around is me. Okay?"

Bumblebee nodded.

"So let's practice. Are you ready?"

Bumblebee nodded again. Charlie took a few steps back to give him some room. "Okay," she said. "If you see anyone besides me, what do you do?"

Apparently very eager to demonstrate he understood Charlie, Bumblebee jumped as he shifted and clicked his robot body back into the form of the Beetle. He landed in the sand and bounced on his tires.

"Good, perfect," Charlie said, stepping back again to put some more distance between her and the Beetle. "Okay, you can change back now."

Again, the Beetle's parts slid back and returned Bumblebee to robot form.

"That was good," Charlie said, "now if we—" She glanced over her shoulder, as if she were gazing past the rocks that surrounded the parking area, and then she said in a loud whisper, "Oh no, someone's here. Hide!" She darted behind a rock and ducked down behind it.

Bumblebee looked at a nearby rock, then mimicked Charlie's action. He jumped over the rock and crouched on the other side of it.

Charlie stood up, looked at the rock that Bumblebee had selected, and then looked at Bumblebee. She could see him clearly. The rock was only a few feet high and did not even begin to hide

Bumblebee's massive body. Charlie put her hands on her hips and said, "Seriously?"

Apparently realizing his mistake, Bumblebee immediately changed back into Beetle form.

"Too late," Charlie said, "you're already dead."

The Beetle's parts shifted and slid back until Bumblebee again appeared before Charlie as a robot. He hung his head low and shook it, looking more than a little ashamed.

"It's okay," Charlie said as she walked toward him. "That's why we're practicing. You'll get the hang of it." She reached up and patted his head. Bumblebee's eyes glowed brighter, and Charlie was pretty sure he was smiling.

Charlie smiled, too. She hadn't felt so happy in years.

She heard a distant noise, the sound of a car's engine, and then she realized the noise was getting louder.

Without hesitation, Bumblebee changed back into a car. Charlie got behind the wheel and made a mental note to pick up her abandoned moped on the way home. She started the engine, and they drove off, leaving the beach. As they traveled back up the dirt road, they saw a green sport-utility vehicle coming from the opposite direction. As the SUV passed by, Charlie glanced at its occupants and guessed they were a family heading for the beach.

She began to wonder how long she could keep Bumblebee a secret. She was certain that if others learned about him, they would try to take him away from her, and maybe even destroy him. She promised herself she wouldn't let that happen.

Chapter 6

The next day, the only thing Charlie wanted to do was enjoy more time with Bumblebee. Remembering their experience at the beach, and how long it had taken her to wash the sand out of her hair, she decided they should go to a different isolated area. With Bumblebee in his Beetle form, they drove again to the outskirts of Brighton Falls, but this time their destination was a forest.

Charlie didn't see any people or parked cars on the dirt road that wrapped around the edge of the forest, so she brought the Beetle to a stop. She got out, taking her backpack with her. She listened and looked both ways to make sure no one was coming, and then she motioned that it was okay for Bumblebee to come out.

The Beetle's parts slid and peeled back until Bumblebee had changed to his robot body. He shifted his weight from one leg to the other before he rose to his full height.

Charlie led Bumblebee away from the road and onto an old trail overgrown with weeds and flowers and surrounded by tall trees. Sunlight filtered down through the upper branches and across the forest floor. The trail extended for almost a hundred feet before it became lost beneath the thick weeds. Charlie and Bumblebee pressed on until they arrived at a clearing.

Charlie said, "I figured you'd want to go someplace where you could stretch out. It must be lousy to be cooped up in a VW all day, right?"

Bumblebee came to a stop on a grassy mound, tilted his head back, and gazed at the sky. Charlie looked at him and noticed how the sunlight beamed off his metal form. She thought he looked spectacular, but then she realized she could more clearly see the many dents, scars, and corroded areas of his body. She reached up to touch a jagged gash above his right leg. "What in the world happened to you?"

Bumblebee looked at her.

"Is there anyone who can help you? Do you have a family?"

Bumblebee cocked his head.

"You know, like a group of people you live with? Mom, dad, siblings? You all love one another? Or drive one another crazy so you can't wait to get away and start a whole new life?"

Bumblebee lowered his head, and Charlie wondered if he'd understood anything she'd said. Then she noticed a broken section on his chest. Bumblebee adjusted his gaze to look down at the same section and emitted a sad buzz.

Charlie pointed to his chest and said, "You want me to try to fix it?"

Bumblebee looked at Charlie. She sensed that he was concerned. She said, "I'll be gentle."

Bumblebee nodded. Charlie guided him to stand beside a tree stump, and she climbed up onto it so she could be closer to his chest. She used her pocketknife's screwdriver to remove his chest plate. Pulling the plate away, she saw that it concealed high-tech machinery, which also appeared damaged.

"Whoa," Charlie said as she inspected Bumblebee's technological components, an intricate mess of cogs, wires, and lights. Although she had hoped she could fix him, she wasn't sure where to begin.

Bumblebee looked down at his innards and emitted another sad buzz. As Charlie continued to examine his mangled bits and pieces, she reached into her backpack and pulled out a can of soda. She cracked it open and took a deep swallow. Then she noticed Bumblebee was watching her with interest. She said, "Is drinking something you can do?" She pulled another soda from her backpack. "Want one?"

Bumblebee took the unopened can. Curious, he began shaking it.

Charlie said, "I wouldn't do—"

Bumblebee cracked the can open, and it exploded with a shower of fizzing liquid. It was still fizzing as he tilted his head back and poured it onto his face. Soda streamed down his metal cheeks and neck and onto his chest. Something in his body made a hissing noise.

"Okay, big guy," Charlie said, "no more of that. I

should've seen that coming." She took his can and then pulled out a rag from her backpack. As she used the rag to wipe him down, her finger hit an object that felt as if it was partially lodged in his chest cavity. "What's this? Hold still, okay?"

Bumblebee held still. Charlie worked her fingers into his chest, feeling her way around the object. She touched something that felt like a switch. As she pressed it, she said, "I think maybe this part is—"

Bumblebee's eyes went vacant, his back arched, and his arms flexed out toward his sides. Startled, Charlie dropped her backpack and jumped off the tree stump. She took a few steps away from Bumblebee. Even though he wasn't moving, she thought his upright, rigid stance made him look more imposing and, admittedly, way more frightening.

A light flipped on in Bumblebee's chest, and his upper torso began humming with energy. The light projected a multicolored beam in front of his chest, and the beam shifted and weaved into something that resembled a three-dimensional shape, a holographic image of a tall red-and-dark-blue robot. He appeared to be a creature like Bumblebee. As Charlie stared at the hologram, a voice boomed out from deep within Bumblebee's body, and Charlie realized the voice belonged to the hologram.

"B-127," the hologram said, "I have received your distress signal. I fear the Decepticons may have intercepted it. Stay safe, soldier. Protect the people of Earth until—"

The hologram froze in midair at the same instant the voice cut out. Bumblebee's eyes focused on the hologram, and he blinked at it. He raised his hand and tried to touch the image of the red-and-blue robot, but the hologram flickered and disappeared. Bumblebee looked sad as he stared at the empty space in the air.

Charlie crept forward. "Are you okay?"

Bumblebee turned away from her and looked up at the sky again.

"Who was that?"

Bumblebee looked back at Charlie.

"Is he…is he your family, Bee?"

Bumblebee lowered his gaze and looked at the grass and the nearby tree stump. Charlie could see that he was thinking, but she couldn't tell if he was confused or troubled. She said, "What's a Decepticon?"

Bumblebee looked at the trees at the edge of the forest, as if he were searching for something. Without warning, his radio began hissing loud static. He reached down to tune it, searching the frequencies for a clear signal, but each channel was garbled.

"I know, it's broken," Charlie said. "It doesn't work."

Bumblebee kept trying. He turned the radio's knobs slowly, first clockwise and then counter-clockwise, but only managed to find more static.

"I can get you a new one," Charlie said. "You want me to get you a new radio that works?"

Bumblebee responded with a nod, but he didn't look very hopeful.

Then it hit her. Charlie could kick herself—she

had a perfectly fine radio back at the garage! They could skip Uncle Hank's—and any Bumblebee-related questions or mishaps like they'd almost had with her mom—and go straight home. She picked up her backpack. As Bumblebee followed her back to the road, she was thinking about the tools she might use to hook him up with a new radio. Could she help him get his voice back? She had no idea, but she knew she had to try.

Chapter 7

Inside the garage, Charlie was in the Corvette, removing its stereo system, while Bumblebee sat in front of the TV, which was playing *The Breakfast Club*. Charlie had watched the movie enough times to know it was almost over. She also knew her mother and Ron had retired for the evening, and she was pretty sure Otis had gone to bed, too, but she still took the precaution of locking the garage's main door. She listened and checked the doors every few minutes to confirm they remained locked.

The Corvette's original radio had been a Wonder Bar, equipped with a selector-bar electronic automatic tuner, the first of its kind, which tuned in listenable stations. But a previous owner had removed the Wonder Bar, and then Charlie had helped her father install a new stereo system with a radio and audiocassette player. As she undid the work she and her dad had done on the Corvette's stereo, she said, "Okay, almost done." She looked over at Bumblebee and noticed he was staring at the TV. On the screen, the actor was raising his fist in the air, and then his image froze.

"No way," Charlie said. "You're actually watching the movie?"

Bumblebee responded by raising his own large fist into the air. Charlie laughed. "You can pop in another video if you want."

Even though Bumblebee's fingers were large, Charlie had noticed that he could manipulate them carefully and also handle delicate objects. So when he tapped a button to eject *The Breakfast Club* from the VCR, and then removed the videocassette and placed it on a stack of others, Charlie was more amused than surprised.

While Charlie kept tinkering with the car radio, Bumblebee thumbed through the stack of videocassettes. The stack included a Vietnam War movie, a horror movie, and a romantic drama, but Bumblebee noticed a cassette with a paper label taped to it. On the label, someone had written, *CHARLIE DIVING REGIONALS.*

Bumblebee inserted that cassette into the VCR. A moment later, the TV screen displayed an image of a young girl wearing a swimsuit and cap, standing on a diving board above a swimming pool. The camera moved closer to the girl's face—it was Charlie, but a few years younger.

The camera pulled back. Bumblebee watched as young Charlie took a deep breath before she leaped and bounced away from the diving board. She executed a double somersault before plunging into the water.

"Nice!" said a man's voice from off camera. "Thatta girl! You're doing great."

Hearing her father's voice from across the room, Charlie almost dropped the stereo component. She turned and looked at the TV screen and saw her younger self in the pool, smiling as she surfaced, waving to the camera.

"Not that one!" Charlie said as she moved fast for the VCR. "Where'd you find that?!" Still clutching the Corvette's stereo, she stopped the video and ejected it. When she looked at Bumblebee, she saw he was cowering away from her like a scolded puppy. "Sorry, I just…I'm done with this, so…" She placed the cassette on a nearby shelf.

Bumblebee looked downcast. Charlie wished she could say something to make him feel better, and then she realized she was still holding the stereo system that she'd pulled from the Corvette. She moved close to Bumblebee's chest, found his broken radio just below his metal rib cage, and popped it out of its socket. Then she placed the new stereo system into his chest, connected it to his wires, and said, "All right, let's see if we've got something."

She turned on the radio. It lit up. She heard a faint noise, and then the sound grew louder and became music. Charlie recognized the song, "Take On Me" by a-ha.

"Ha!" Charlie said. *"Yessss!"*

Bumblebee began to sway a little, moving with the music.

"Ah," Charlie said, "you like that, huh?"

Bumblebee answered with a buzzing noise and then swiveled his hips.

Charlie laughed. "You got some moves!" She turned to a box of music cassette tapes and dug through it until she found the one by The Smiths. "Oh, you're gonna dig this," she said as she pushed the cassette into the player in Bumblebee's chest.

A mournful song began playing. Bumblebee listened to it for a few seconds, then ejected the cassette from his chest with such force that it shot across the garage like a missile and smashed into the far wall.

"Okay," Charlie said, "maybe not a Smiths fan." She grabbed a cassette for a hard rock band from the box. "Try this." She popped the cassette into Bumblebee's chest.

The cassette hadn't even started to play when Bumblebee shot it across the garage.

"Okay, not that, either," Charlie said. As she rummaged through the box of cassettes, Bumblebee looked around the garage and noticed a group of boxy objects resting on a shelf. The objects were part of an old stereo system that included a record turntable with a transparent plastic cover, a receiver, and a pair of large speakers. All were covered by a fine layer of dust. Looking to the shelf below the stereo system, Bumblebee saw a neatly organized collection of record albums in cardboard sleeves. He started reaching for the records when Charlie yelled, "Don't touch those!"

Bumblebee cringed, and Charlie felt terrible for having shouted at him again. She moved closer to him, pointed to the record albums, and said, "They belonged to my dad."

Bumblebee cocked his head.

"They're records. You put them on that thing." Charlie pointed to the record player that rested between the two speakers.

Bumblebee leaned in to study the record player's circular turntable. He examined the thin, articulated arm that extended beside the turntable. He touched the arm and then lifted it up and down. Moving one finger beneath the arm's end, he found a sharp point, the tone arm's diamond stylus. He poked at the machine, trying to figure out how it worked.

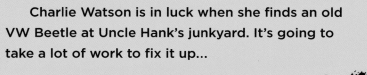

Charlie Watson is in luck when she finds an old VW Beetle at Uncle Hank's junkyard. It's going to take a lot of work to fix it up...

...but she does it! Charlie is the proud owner of her very own car, and she drives it off the lot.

As Charlie starts to fix up the car, she notices that something's not quite right. It has parts in places no car Charlie's ever worked on before has had parts. A mysterious arm-shaped...thing...falls off while she is poking around.

Charlie investigates, shining a bright light in search of the mystery part.

Suddenly, instead of a car, Charlie is face-to-face with a twelve-foot-tall robot!

But the robot huddles in the corner, unsure of how he got into a strange garage.

The robot's name is Bumblebee.

Charlie and her friend Memo look on as Bumblebee leaps into action.

Trouble is on the horizon. Agent Burns and a government organization are hunting down Bumblebee.

Shatter and Dropkick, Decepticon Rangers, are also hunting Bumblebee. They race through the desert in hot pursuit.

Bumblebee is on the run.

Bumblebee and Charlie bond. He wants to help Charlie the best he can.

And that means protecting her when his pursuers catch wind of him.

Together, Charlie and Bumblebee make a plan.
They're in for the adventure of their lives!

Charlie could tell Bumblebee was fascinated by the record player. "All right," she said, "we'll listen to this *one*. Okay? So you can see how it works." She selected an album by Sam Cooke, removed the vinyl disc from its sleeve, and placed it on the turntable. She pressed a switch. The turntable began rotating, and then she moved the tone arm so its stylus rested against the disc's outer edge. Music began playing from two speakers, and then Bumblebee heard a man's voice singing.

Bumblebee was soon mesmerized by the sound of the music and Cooke's voice. Charlie could see his entire body relax, and then he began swaying again, feeling the music.

"Ah, you finally approve," Charlie said. She looked at the album cover. "Good taste. This was my dad's favorite, too. That's him, there." She pointed to a Polaroid photo of her father that was thumbtacked above the workbench.

Bumblebee glanced at the photo, then looked around the garage. He cocked his head as he lowered his gaze to Charlie, and she realized he was wondering where her father was. She said, "Oh, he's not here."

Bumblebee cocked his head again.

"We don't need to talk about it."

Bumblebee didn't respond to that. He started to survey the garage's interior again, but then Charlie said, "He passed away a few years ago. Heart attack."

Charlie couldn't tell if Bumblebee understood, but something in his eyes conveyed that he was sympathetic. She gestured to the rusted-out Corvette. "See that car? He loved it. We used to work on it together every weekend. It was gonna be mine one day."

Bumblebee looked at the Corvette and the pieces of its engine scattered around.

"I really wanted to finish it," Charlie said, "just hear it start up, you know? Be able to say, *Hey, Dad, we did it. We finally did it.*" She felt tears welling up in her eyes. "I don't know. It's dumb."

Bumblebee moved closer. He reached out and patted her head, his touch so gentle that she almost didn't feel it. They'd reached an unspoken agreement: Bumblebee understood that Charlie wanted to take care of him, and she suspected that he wanted to take care of her, too.

After leaving his job at the churro stand, Memo rode his bicycle home. As he skidded to a stop in his driveway, he glanced at the house where the girl next door lived. He noticed lights on in the garage, and also odd, muffled noises. Curious, he popped his kickstand and walked closer to the garage.

He heard footsteps and turned to see a neighbor, an older man that Memo didn't know by name, walking his dog. Fearing that the man might mistake him for a prowler, Memo turned his attention to a nearby bush and said, "This plant is nice, what is this?"

The man shook his head, said, "I don't know anything about plants," and kept walking, taking his dog with him.

Memo let out a long exhale. Then he heard more noises from the garage. It sounded like fragmented bursts of music and voices. He wondered if someone was playing with a radio, whipping through random stations. He wondered why anyone would do that. Interesting. Very interesting.

Inside the garage, Charlie watched with amazement as the tone-control knob and the manual tuning knob on Bumblebee's new radio rotated on their own. As the knobs turned, the station selector bar shifted back and forth, and Bumblebee's speakers released a stream of garbled noise.

"I know there are a lot of choices, man," Charlie said, "but you gotta pick a station."

Bumblebee continued to scan every frequency he could find and kept blasting bits of music until Charlie couldn't stand it anymore. She reached for the tuning knob and tried to lock in one station, but Bumblebee gently swatted her away.

"Sorry," Charlie said. "Didn't mean to get handsy."

The radio's knobs continued rotating back and forth. Charlie wondered if Bumblebee was searching for one station in particular. She leaned in closer to the radio and said, "What are you trying to—?"

Charlie heard a loud gasp from behind her and then a loud clatter. She spun around and saw a teenage boy with frizzy black hair standing in the garage's side doorway. The boy's mouth hung open, and he'd just accidentally knocked over a bunch of garden shovels.

Charlie realized she'd left the garage's side door open and felt like kicking herself. She also vaguely recognized the boy....

Bumblebee saw the boy, too. Charlie hoped Bumblebee would remember what she'd told him about strangers, about changing into car form. But because the boy had seen him, she wasn't sure what he should do. She sensed Bumblebee was just as flustered as he stepped away from her to give himself more space, then changed into a car as fast as he could.

The boy locked his wide-eyed gaze on the yellow Beetle. He began stammering, but clearly he was so frightened that the words wouldn't come out. Charlie moved in front of him and said, "Just please don't scream, okay?"

The boy's jaw began shaking. He looked as if he

actually was about to scream, so Charlie clamped her hand over his mouth. The boy's entire body began trembling instead, so Charlie removed her hand from his face. "Sit down," she said. "Breathe."

Still shaking, the boy sat down on an overturned bucket. He looked as if he was going to be ill. He stammered out, "Was that...did I...what the—?"

"First of all, hi," Charlie said, trying her best to sound calm. "I'm Charlie." She extended her hand to him.

Dazed, the boy looked at her hand for a moment, then took it, shook it, and said, "Memo."

"Nice to meet you."

Memo's eyes flicked to the Beetle and then back to Charlie. "Pleasure's all mine," he said, but his fear was evident in his voice.

"Look," Charlie said, "I know what you just saw is a little crazy. I can explain it. Well, I can't explain it, but here's the deal. If you tell anyone...I will run you over with my car."

Memo whimpered and said, "Really?"

"No, not *really*," Charlie said. "I just need nobody else to know. All right?"

Memo nodded.

"You promise?"

Memo nodded again.

"You can come out, Bumblebee."

Memo gasped as the Beetle changed back into a robot. Bumblebee looked at Memo and took a step back, apparently uncertain of how to behave around a new person.

"Wow," Memo said. "It's...wow. What is it?"

"Not *it*," Charlie said. "*He*. Don't worry, he won't hurt you."

"Wow," Memo said again. "Before tonight, I was having the most boring summer."

Chapter 8

It was the day after Charlie installed the radio into Bumblebee, and Bumblebee was still in the garage, still turning the knobs on his radio and scanning one station after another. Charlie remained baffled about what he was trying to accomplish, but she could tell from the way he kept studying the radio that it was somehow very important to him.

She heard a knock at the garage's side door. She was expecting Memo, so she went to the door and opened it. Memo walked in, looked at Bumblebee, and then looked back at Charlie and said, "Okay, I've been up all night, figuring it out, and I've got it. I know exactly what he is."

"Really?" Charlie said, surprised. She looked at Bumblebee, who had also heard Memo and was now looking at the boy with interest. "Okay, Memo, tell us."

But Memo looked unsure if Bumblebee should

hear what he had to say. He pulled Charlie aside and whispered, "All right. He...he's a sentient robot from an alien planet full of other sentient robots, and there are good ones and bad ones, and they fight and have wars, and they change into cars when they need a disguise."

Charlie nodded, urging Memo to continue.

"What he is," Memo said, "is a GoBot."

"A GoBot?" Charlie said. "Like the kids' toy? No, he's not a GoBot."

Memo reached into his back pocket and pulled out a rolled-up comic book. He unrolled it and showed the illustrated cover to Charlie. The title was *GoBot Adventures*.

"Look at this," Memo said, pointing to a robot on the cover. "Doesn't that look like him?"

Charlie studied the illustration, then looked at Bumblebee and said, "Not exactly."

"Close, though, right?"

Bumblebee shuffled on his feet. Charlie looked again at the comic book. *"Ehh."*

"I'm telling you, that's what he is." Memo noticed Bumblebee tinkering with the radio's knobs and said, "What's he doing? Going up and down the dial like that?"

"I don't know," Charlie said, "but he's been doing it all night."

"He's trying to get a message to his people!" Memo said with conviction. He moved closer to Bumblebee, gazed into his eyes, and said, "GoBot phone home?"

Bumblebee jerked his head back and gave Memo a sidelong glance, as if Memo had just said something crazy. Then Charlie heard the muffled voices of her mother and Otis coming from inside the house. Worried they might try walking into the garage, she looked at Memo and said, "Come on, let's get him out of here."

In an instant, Bumblebee transformed back into a car. Memo hopped into the passenger seat, and Charlie opened the garage door and started the engine. Leaving the cul-de-sac, they kept to the back roads of Brighton Falls until they arrived on a road that took them along the ocean shore. As they traveled, Bumblebee continued adjusting the radio's control knobs, scanning through stations, and Charlie tried to bring Memo up to speed. It was a tougher task than she thought.

Memo said, "So tell me everything about this hologram you saw."

"It looked like *him*," Charlie said as she tapped the Beetle's dashboard, "but red and blue, and it had a deep voice and said something like, *Stay safe, soldier. Protect the people of Earth.*"

"Really?" Memo looked out the window as they passed a row of beach houses, and looked nervous. He looked back at Charlie. "What...what if there's gonna be an invasion? There's gotta be somebody we can call. Is Area 51 in the phone book?"

"No, we can't tell anyone," Charlie said. "We can *never* tell anyone. It's just you and me. That's it. Forever."

"Sure," Memo agreed. "Okay. You and me." He looked thoughtful as he watched the road ahead. Turning to Charlie, he said, "Then maybe we should just...you know...go somewhere for a while. Where we can be alone. The two of us."

The Beetle's engine made a coughing, grinding noise that sounded like an objection. Memo tapped the Beetle's dashboard and said, "I mean, the *three* of us."

As if in response, the Beetle's speakers blared out the voice of Olivia Newton-John, who sang, *"Physical. Let's get into physical. Let me hear your body talk."*

Hearing the song, Charlie cracked up. She assumed Bumblebee had accidentally played the song, but she couldn't help laughing—it seemed as if he was making fun of Memo with his song selection. "Well played, Bee," Charlie said.

Charlie and Memo stared at the radio, then looked at each other. Charlie returned her gaze to the radio and said, "Whoa, wait. Is that why you're always messing with the dial, Bee? Are you teaching yourself to talk?"

Bumblebee readjusted the dial to play the lyrics from a song by the Four Seasons. *"Walk like a man, talk like a man."*

"No freaking way," Memo said.

"Bee, you're a genius," Charlie said. "An actual genius!"

They were heading for Markham Point, a long

stretch of beach with high, rocky cliffs. As they rounded a bend, they found a bunch of cars parked beside the road, and then they saw several more cars parked at odd angles in the road, blocking their way. As Charlie slowed the Beetle to a stop, she said, "Oh, come on. Really?"

And then she recognized some of the parked cars. They belonged to the Pretty Mean Girls from high school. And then she remembered that her former friends Brenda and Liz had mentioned Tina Lark's bonfire party and realized that's why so many kids had gathered at the beach. Perfect.

Memo rolled down his window. He waved to a small crowd of teens who were standing in the road in front of the Beetle, and he tried to sound polite as he said, "Excuse me, we need to get through."

Everyone ignored him. Charlie leaned on the horn. The party crowd responded by yelling at her to stop honking.

Memo looked at Charlie. "We need to go ask someone to move." He quickly opened his door and got out.

Charlie brushed her fingers along the edge of the radio and said, "Bee, I promise we'll be right back, okay? Don't do anything crazy." She got out of the Beetle and started walking toward the people and cars blocking the road. She'd taken only a few steps when she walked right into two girls who were so overdressed, in outfits that included leg warmers, that she almost didn't recognize them. But then she did. "Brenda? Liz?"

"Oh…hey," Liz said, turning to face Charlie.

Charlie said, "What are you doing here?"

Brenda glanced at Liz. Liz shrugged and said, "Tina invited us."

"Tina Lark?" Charlie shook her head. "Why would she do that? She hates you guys. She hates all of us."

Liz shrugged again. "I guess she changed her—"

"We give her free corn dogs," Brenda said.

Liz shot Brenda an angry look. Brenda bit her lower lip and looked at the ground.

Stunned, Charlie said, "You give her free corn dogs so she'll be friends with you?"

Liz said, "It's not that big of a—"

"Hot dog girls!" shouted a guy as he broke away from the crowd. He threw his arms around Brenda and Liz. Then the guy jumped away and began a silly dance, mimicking the movements of a lemonade churner.

Annoyed with the guy, Liz said, "Come on, let's go, Brenda."

As Liz and Brenda walked off, Charlie saw Memo standing beside the Beetle. She went over to him and saw that he was looking at another group of teens, which had gathered at the edge of one cliff. Memo said, "What are they doing?"

Leaning against the side of the Beetle, Charlie scanned the group just as one guy was pulling off his shirt. She said, "Is that Tripp Summers?" And then the guy turned around. He was indeed Tripp Summers, and he was stripping down to his boxers.

Tripp leaned out to look over the cliff's edge. Someone said, "Don't do it, dude. You're crazy."

Tripp said, "Ah, it's not that big of a jump."

Someone else shouted, "Hey, Tripp's gonna wreck himself! Everyone come watch!"

As the crowd moved up closer to Tripp, he grinned at his audience and said, "Doesn't *anyone* want to go with me?"

"You're on your own, man," said another partygoer.

"Anybody?" Tripp said. "Come on, people, live a little! Isn't there anyone else with the guts to jump off this thing?" He looked around.

Charlie was still leaning against the Beetle when Bumblebee flexed and opened the door behind her, pushing her forward. She stumbled toward the crowd near Tripp.

Tripp saw her and said, "Ah-ha! One brave volunteer!"

Charlie realized Tripp was addressing her and didn't understand why until she glanced back and saw the Beetle's door swing shut. Facing Tripp, she said, "No, I didn't mean to—"

The Beetle's radio blared, *"You got the touch. You got the power. Yeah!"*

Tripp squinted at Charlie and said, "Hey, wait a minute. I know you."

Charlie assumed that he remembered her as the

girl who spilled lemonade all over him. She said, "Yeah, I'm sorry about that, I—"

"You were on the dive team with my little sister. I saw you win state a couple of years ago."

"Oh," Charlie said. "Uh…"

Tripp beamed. "Girls and boys, we've got a champion high diver here. This just got a lot more interesting!"

The crowd cheered. Tina Lark rolled her eyes with distaste.

Facing Charlie, Tripp said, "Don't worry. I won't make you go first." Then he moved fast and took a running leap off the edge. Instead of diving, he clasped his knees to his chest and executed a sloppy cannonball, hitting the water with a big splash.

The crowd hooted and hollered at Tripp. His head popped up from the water, and he shouted, "Oh wow, that's cold!" He looked at Charlie. "You better not back out!"

Charlie looked around. Everyone was staring at her, waiting for her to follow Tripp into the ocean.

She glanced down at the water and saw Tripp bobbing and waving to her. Someone started chanting, "Dive, dive, dive," and then the entire crowd took on the chant. They chanted louder and louder.

Charlie closed her eyes. From out of nowhere, she thought she heard her father's voice say, *Thatta girl.* Her eyes snapped open. Had she imagined her father's voice? Had Bumblebee somehow recorded it from the videotape and played it back on his radio? She didn't know. But she did know she wasn't going to dive.

She walked away from the edge. The crowd began to boo. She returned to the Beetle, where Memo was waiting for her. Memo said, "You okay?"

"Let's just go."

Before they could climb back into the Beetle, Tina and her girlfriends swarmed around them. Tina moved up close to Charlie and said, "Where're you going, sweetie? What happened out there?" She gestured to the diving spot on the cliff. "That was your big moment to look cool."

Memo scowled at Tina and said, "Move out of the way. We're leaving."

Tina looked at Memo as if he were an insignificant thing. "Who's that?" she said. "Is that the churro guy? Where's your hairnet, dude?"

"In the garbage, Einstein," Memo said. "You throw them away after each use." Then he looked at Charlie and said, "That was a weird comeback, and I regret it."

Facing Tina, Charlie said, "Just get out of the way, okay?"

Tina looked at Charlie's messy hair. "Nice haircut. What's it called? Let me guess: *Cry for help*?"

The Beetle's parts began to shift. Charlie appreciated that Bumblebee was probably hoping to protect her from Tina and the other girls, but she placed her hand on his hood to calm him down.

Tina and her friends ripped into Charlie and Memo, taunting them about their clothes and how they looked. Charlie and Memo got into the Beetle, but the girls continued standing in front of them. Charlie shouted, "Move! Please!" The girls didn't budge.

Bumblebee apparently couldn't stand the mean girls anymore. He activated his horn, blasting it at them. But the horn took Charlie and Memo by surprise, too, causing them to jump in their seats. Charlie looked at the button for the horn on the steering wheel, then she looked at Memo and said, "That's not me. I'm not doing that."

Bumblebee floored the accelerator, and the Beetle leaped forward.

Charlie said, "Bee, no, no, no!"

The group of girls in front of the car screamed and shrieked and jumped out of the way. The Beetle raced off past them. Memo glanced back through the Beetle's rear window as the girls were flipping out, yelling and pointing at the departing car. Memo shrugged and said, "That's what happens when you annoy a GoBot." He looked at Charlie. "You all right?"

"I'm fine."

"They're idiots," Memo said. As they drove on and away from the beach, heading back into town, Charlie was still annoyed and rattled by her encounter with Tina. Picking up on that, Memo said, "I know what would make you feel better."

Charlie shot him a quick look. "Oh?"

"Revenge."

"No," Charlie said, "I don't want revenge."

"I do. What about you, Bee?"

From his radio, Bumblebee responded with James Brown singing, *"Revenge! The big pay-back! Woo!"*

"Two against one," Memo said with a sly smile. They were approaching a shopping plaza with a supermarket. He pointed to the plaza and said, "Come on; I got an idea."

In a shadowy bunker, Shatter and Dropkick were executing their own plan. B-127 was not only known by the humans, but their pitiful military was looking for him. It didn't matter to the sinister robots why. Shatter suggested an alliance with the leader of the organization, a man called Burns, after calming Dropkick's shortsighted lust for violence. Using the resources of "friends" would make their search significantly easier, and if it was easier to concoct a story about B-127's capacity for global annihilation for some pathetic humans, so be it. When they located and cornered their prey, nothing, not even their temporary allies, would stop them from getting what they wanted.

Chapter 9

Charlie and Memo waited until dark to drive the Beetle over to Tina Lark's neighborhood. They couldn't help but notice that the houses were much larger and more expensive than those in the area where they lived, and most of them had expansive lawns with ornamental shrubs. They parked around the corner from Tina's house, on a street bordered by tall hedges and without streetlights. Charlie and Memo climbed out of the Beetle, taking the packages of toilet paper and bagged cartons of eggs that they'd bought at the supermarket. Bumblebee waited for them to step away before he shifted into robot form.

They moved as quietly as they could, staying on the grassy stretches along the edge of the street so Bumblebee's metal feet would make little noise. They came to a stop in front of Tina's enormous house and saw Tina's car, with its roof up, parked in the driveway. Looking at the convertible, Charlie had second thoughts about the eggs she was carrying. She said, "I think there's a rule about doing this after the age of twelve."

"There's a bigger rule," Memo said, "called *don't bottle your anger*. Let's show Bee what to do." Memo ripped open a shrink-wrapped pack of twenty-four rolls of toilet paper and handed a roll to Charlie.

"See this, Bee?" Charlie said, holding up a roll. "It's toilet paper. It's for when you—" Charlie tried to think of how she might explain the purpose of the rolls of paper to Bumblebee but decided she wasn't up for the challenge. "Never mind. Just take a roll."

Bumblebee reached out and gently plucked the roll from Charlie's hand. He held the roll between one large metal thumb and forefinger and crushed it.

"No, no, no," Charlie said, "you *throw* it. Like this." She grabbed another roll, brought her arm back, then tossed the roll high into the air so it unfurled across the branches of a tree next to Tina's driveway.

Bumblebee observed Charlie's action and nodded. Then he picked up the pack that held the remaining rolls and threw the entire thing so hard that it sailed over Tina's house and vanished into the night sky. Apparently pleased with how well he had thrown the pack, Bumblebee pumped up his chest and beamed at Charlie.

Charlie was not so impressed. Before she could comment, Memo held up a carton of eggs, looked at Bumblebee, and said, "How about you be the egg man?" He pointed to Tina's convertible and said, "Here, that's your bull's-eye."

Memo demonstrated by hurling an egg at the parked car. The egg smacked and splatted across the windshield.

Charlie removed an egg from the carton and held it out for Bumblebee. As he reached for it, Charlie said, "You gotta be really careful with these. They're super—"

Bumblebee's fingers crushed the egg, and its gooey contents dripped down from his fingertips.

"—fragile," Charlie said. "That's okay." She handed him another egg.

Bumblebee tried to be more careful, but he broke the second egg, too. Frustrated, he took the entire carton from Charlie and carried it up the driveway. He stopped beside the convertible and loomed over it. He held the carton above the car's soft roof, squeezed his fingers closed, and crushed the carton. Sticky gobs of yolks and albumen oozed from his fist and dripped onto the roof.

Charlie laughed and said, "That works, too."

Pleased that he'd made Charlie laugh, Bumblebee looked eager to do some more damage to the convertible. So he raised one foot and smashed it down on the car, crushing it against the driveway, and then he brought his foot down on it again and again.

Charlie gasped. "What are you doing?!"

Bumblebee looked at the remains of the convertible, which he had reduced to an unrecognizable wreck, then he looked at Charlie. Seeing her astonished expression, he looked as if he wondered if he had done something wrong. As he stepped away from the wreck, the convertible's alarm began wailing. A moment later, a light came on in a window of Tina's house.

"Hide!" Charlie said.

Memo grabbed Charlie's arm and pulled her behind a bush. Bumblebee looked for a bush that was large enough for him to hide behind but couldn't find anything. He reached down to the wrecked BMW, grabbed it, flipped it onto its side, and then crouched behind it with his hands covering his head.

Charlie saw Bumblebee and rolled her eyes with disbelief. Memo said, "We gotta get out of here!"

Charlie and Memo ducked down and ran toward Bumblebee. He jumped away from the wreckage, letting it fall and crash against the driveway as he tumbled, shifted, and changed into Beetle form. He opened the front doors, Charlie and Memo jumped in, and they raced away from Tina's house as fast as they could.

Sheriff Lock sat in his parked police cruiser and tried hard not to be bored. It was a quiet night in Brighton Falls, so quiet that Lock held his radar gun outside the car's window and pretended to shoot it as if it were a ray gun. The police dispatcher, Lucy, had told him that she'd heard about a beach party at Markham Point and that he should keep his eyes peeled for teenagers leaving that area. But after sitting in his cruiser for over an hour and seeing only a few cars go by, and each one going at or under the speed limit, he radioed in and said, "Lucy, this is stupid. There's no one—"

A loud engine roared from behind Sheriff Lock's cruiser, and then a yellow Beetle flashed past him. The noise so completely startled Lock that he dropped his radar gun, which registered the Beetle's speed at seventy miles per hour. He fumbled with the ignition, stomped on the accelerator, and took off in pursuit.

Charlie looked in the Beetle's rearview mirror and saw red and blue lights flashing. Memo must have seen the lights, too, because he said, "Uh-oh."

Charlie could imagine how her mother would

react if she got a speeding ticket, and she knew her mother would be even more outraged if the police discovered that Charlie was somehow involved with the destruction of Tina Lark's convertible. But she knew what she'd done was wrong, and she also knew better than to try to run from the cops. She tapped the brake, and the Beetle started to slow down.

But Bumblebee must have seen the red and blue lights on the vehicle behind him, and his instincts must have told him that meant trouble, the kind he should avoid. He ignored Charlie's foot on the brake pedal and accelerated down the road, away from any potential danger.

Surprised, Charlie said, "What are you doing, Bee?"

Bumblebee increased speed, racing faster over the dark road.

Charlie shouted, "What are you doing?!"

The road narrowed, and Bumblebee began navigating a series of sharp curves that snaked along and above the coastal cliffs. Fifty feet below the road, waves crashed against the rocky shore. Charlie and Memo clutched at their seat belts as the Beetle wrapped around a corner.

Bumblebee came up on an old, slow-moving pickup truck. He slowed down, but the police cruiser was still behind him and catching up. As the pickup approached a hairpin bend, Bumblebee accelerated again and shot past the pickup, just barely avoiding it. He hit the shoulder and sprayed gravel before fishtailing, sending his back tires over the cliff's edge. Charlie and Memo screamed.

The Beetle's left side wobbled over a sheer drop. Charlie and Memo were still screaming as Bumblebee deployed an arm from his undercarriage to stabilize himself and keep him on the road. He gunned his engine, scooted all four tires back onto the road, and raced forward, heading for the dark mouth of a tunnel.

Charlie glanced back and saw the police cruiser had managed to get around the slow pickup. The cruiser was gaining on them as Bumblebee sped into the tunnel. Looking ahead, Charlie noticed they were in the straightaway for the Pico Tunnel, a tubular passage with curved walls that wrapped up into a long, curved ceiling.

With its siren blaring, the cruiser sped into the tunnel and began to move up alongside the Beetle. As the cruiser approached, Bumblebee rapidly lowered his front seats, dropping Charlie and Memo so they disappeared from view below the windows.

As Sheriff Lock drew up beside the Beetle, he *definitely* noticed that no one was seated behind its steering wheel. Bumblebee barely made out his panicked voice: "What in the—?!" Lock said, and grabbed his radio. "Lucy, we've got a Code... We've got a yellow car driving itself through the Pico Tunnel!"

Obviously believing the Beetle was out of control and it was up to him to stop it, Lock rammed his cruiser into the Beetle's side, forcing it up sideways against the tunnel's curved wall. Sparks flew as the Beetle connected with concrete and the cruiser.

Bumblebee angled his tires to grab the wall and

allowed the cruiser to push him higher until all his tires were off the road and on the wall. The cruiser accelerated and moved up past the Beetle. As the cruiser raced ahead of him in the tunnel, Bumblebee accelerated, too, gripping the wall as he used his momentum to carry him higher. Still traveling on the wall, he adjusted his form as he pushed off the wall, launching himself up and over the cruiser. In midair, and at seventy miles an hour, Bumblebee half shifted his form into a robot, taking care to protect Charlie and Memo. He flipped and landed on the cruiser's hood, his foot smashing the front of the vehicle.

Sheriff Lock shouted as he saw a yellow-and-black robot crash down on the front of his cruiser. The cruiser jounced, and as Lock swerved to a stop, Bumblebee waved as he drove out of sight.

Back on the road, Bumblebee shifted into Beetle mode and increased speed again. When he shot out of the tunnel, he was traveling at 120 miles per hour. He approached a curve and decelerated to the speed limit, then he adjusted the front seats, lifting them so Charlie and Memo were upright again. They looked out through the windshield at the road ahead. Memo said, "Are we alive? We're alive, right?"

"I think so," Charlie said, gasping.

"I didn't see grandparents or a white light," Memo said, "but I'm still not totally positive we're not dead."

Charlie pushed her hair out of her face. "I think we're okay."

"Okay, cool. Can I ask you a question?"

"Sure."

"Where's the nearest place that sells pants, and can we go there?"

Charlie laughed. Memo shook his head, and then he began laughing, too.

Sheriff Lock felt dazed and dumbfounded as he drove his damaged cruiser at a slow crawl through the tunnel. When he finally exited and came to a stop, he was still wondering about what he'd just witnessed. He looked around. The Beetle was gone, and the robot was nowhere in sight.

He knew he would have a difficult time describing what had happened in the tunnel, but he was certain the Beetle wasn't an ordinary car. He'd seen it change with his own eyes. He was sure of that.

His radio squawked, and then he heard Lucy say, "Update on the vehicle, sir?"

"Uh…" Lock said, still shaken, "the vehicle…the vehicle…turned into a robot and drove away on the ceiling going about one-twenty."

The radio was silent for a few seconds, and then Lucy said, "License plate number?"

Bumblebee maintained the speed limit for the rest of the night and delivered Charlie and Memo to their cul-de-sac without drawing any more attention to himself. After dropping off Memo in front of his house, Bumblebee remained in Beetle mode as Charlie parked him in her garage.

Charlie patted the Beetle's hood.

Bumblebee flashed the Beetle's parking lights.

G'night, Bee, Charlie thought before she left the garage. Entering the kitchen, she almost tripped over Otis's skateboard. As she picked up the skateboard and propped it up next to the door, she looked around the kitchen and then at the living room. Everything looked so familiar and boring. Her mother and Ron had talked about redecorating the house eventually, but Charlie couldn't imagine how new furniture and appliances would change her opinion of the place. And if they ever did get around to redecorating, she hoped she and Bumblebee would be long gone from Brighton Falls by then.

But as she got into bed, and she thought about Tina Lark's ruined car and the escape from the police cruiser, she began to realize that keeping Bumblebee, and keeping him a secret, was a bigger challenge than she'd imagined. A little bit of boring before she got out of town might go a long way.

Yeah, right.

As Charlie worried about Bumblebee and tried to sleep, Bumblebee's worst nightmare was coming true in another state. A shadowy organization had finally made contact with other Cybertronians. The Decepticons had acquired a dangerous new ally.

Chapter 10

It was early morning at Charlie's house. Ron had left for work, and Sally and Otis were in the kitchen, finishing breakfast. Otis was wearing his karate uniform. The toaster on the counter popped up something black. Charlie swept through the kitchen, grabbed her extra-crispy breakfast, and went out the door to the garage.

She found the Beetle resting next to the unfinished Corvette. She moved beside the Beetle and patted the hood. "I gotta go to work, okay? You're gonna stay here."

Bumblebee opened the driver's door, inviting Charlie to climb in.

"No," Charlie said firmly. "After last night, you're grounded, buddy."

The Beetle emitted a sad mechanical noise.

"Look, you've gotta stay in the garage now. After what happened, I'm pretty sure the cops are gonna be looking for you. And no offense, but you don't exactly blend in." Charlie closed the driver's door and planted a kiss on the Beetle's roof. She gestured to the nearby TV and VCR to give Bumblebee permission to dig in and said, "I'll be back soon. I promise."

Charlie climbed onto her moped, scooted out of the garage, and rode away, heading for her job at the hot dog stand.

Several minutes later, Sally and Otis were in the station wagon, on the way to drop Otis off at karate. They had no idea that they'd also left Conan in the company of a living robot disguised as a Volkswagen Beetle.

Still in Beetle mode, Bumblebee was watching a movie on the TV in the garage when he heard a noise from the door that connected to Charlie's house. He directed his gaze to the bottom of the door, where a plastic flap opened. Then Conan pushed his way through the flap and into the garage.

Conan walked over to the Beetle. He sniffed at one of the Beetle's front tires and then started whining. He was still whining as he walked away, heading back the way he'd entered. He pushed his head against the plastic flap and vanished into the house.

Intrigued, Bumblebee changed into robot form and crawled across the garage floor so he could examine the mysterious plastic flap. He pushed it open and peered through. He saw Conan on the other side, looking back at him. Conan whined again. Looking beyond Conan, Bumblebee could make out a small area of the kitchen.

Conan walked away, leaving Bumblebee's view. Bumblebee strained against the small opening in the door, trying to see more and find the dog. He felt a mechanism shift in his head and was surprised when a retractable visor clicked down over his face. He was even more surprised when the visor broke up his vision into dozens of hexagonal cells, increasing his range of vision and enabling him to see more of the house's interior.

He zoomed in on individual cells. He saw a big

console television in a living room. Another cell displayed framed photos hanging on a wall, photos of Charlie and her family. Another cell offered a view of a window, and Bumblebee could see through the window and beyond it, to the birds outside, and the ocean, and—

The door that Bumblebee had been leaning on creaked, snapped from its hinges, and collapsed onto the kitchen floor. Bumblebee emitted a guilty-sounding buzz as he examined the wrecked door. But because he was curious and also knew that he and Conan were alone in the house, he decided to look around some more.

He was still viewing multiple hexagonal cells through his visor as he squeezed through the open doorway and into the kitchen. He saw a rectangular table with chairs made of wood and tubular steel. He also saw that the kitchen had a high ceiling, with crisscrossing wooden beams. He stood up and accidentally bumped his head on a light fixture. His vision-enhancing visor automatically retracted into his head, and he jerked his neck back in surprise.

He wondered where Conan had gone and began

to explore the kitchen. He was fascinated by the shapes and possible uses for various objects on the shelves of a tall buffet that extended up to the ceiling. He saw a can of soda on a counter. Remembering the day he and Charlie had visited a clearing in a nearby forest, and how he'd tried opening a similar can but somehow caused its fizzy contents to explode, he kept his distance.

He moved on to the living room. He thought he was being careful, but he failed to notice he was leaving a trail of damaged floor tiles and scratched woodwork.

An enormous sofa was positioned in front of the big console television and a fireplace. Bumblebee shuffled around the sofa and tried to sit on it. The sofa's legs snapped beneath his weight, and its entire frame collapsed.

He got up from the ruined sofa and made his way back to the kitchen, where he began examining electrical appliances and assorted gadgets. He leaned in close to study a coffee maker with a built-in analog clock. He extended a finger, and a tiny metallic probe popped out from the end of it. He maneuvered the probe against the clock's metal hands and began spinning them.

The coffee machine made a loud *ping*. Bumblebee didn't expect it to produce the sudden burst of hot water that struck the machine's hot plate with a hissing noise. Frightened, he grabbed the coffee machine and yanked it off the counter. The machine's power cord popped out of its electrical socket in the wall.

Bumblebee was relieved that the machine stopped working. He noticed the black plastic cord that dangled from the machine's side. Just then, Conan wandered into the kitchen, whining. Bumblebee looked at Conan's tail, then looked again at the machine's plastic cord, which wasn't moving at all. He wondered what the cord was for.

He glanced at the other small appliances, a toaster and a blender, which were also on the counter. He saw that their plastic cords were plugged into sockets in the wall. He also noticed a socket with nothing plugged into it. He was still holding the coffeemaker with one hand as he reached out with his other and extended the metal probe on the end of his giant finger and pushed the probe into the socket.

Electricity surged into Bumblebee's hand, causing it to glow white with energy... and also causing eight city blocks to lose power. Bumblebee's entire body shook and rattled, and a strange green energy flowed out from his hand and into the household circuitry. The socket in front of his finger exploded with sparks. He fell over backward onto the floor, crushing the tiles beneath him. He was out cold.

As he lay sprawled across the damaged floor, the green energy traveled along the house's wiring and branched up and out. One branch went down and around through a series of breakers until it entered the back of the refrigerator. Other branches flooded into more large and small appliances.

The refrigerator started shuddering. The dishwasher began rocking back and forth. Loud noises came from the closet where the washer and dryer were. The big console television flickered on and off.

And then the appliances really came to life.

Memo was climbing onto his bike, about to ride off to his summer job, when he heard the sound of smashing glass from inside Charlie's house. He knew Charlie was at work and was pretty sure the rest of her family wasn't at home, either, but he also knew that Charlie had left Bumblebee in the garage. So when he heard more smashing noises, he was more than curious. He was worried.

He scooted his bike over to Charlie's house, left the bike near the front door, and crept up near the kitchen window. He flinched as something crashed inside the house. Nervous, he peeked through the window.

"Oh no," he said. "Oh-no-oh-no." He jumped away from the window and sprinted back to his house. Once inside, he ran to his living room, grabbed the telephone, and started dialing.

Charlie was refilling the ketchup containers at the hot dog stand when her supervisor, Craig, stuck his head out his office door and said, "You have a personal call." He didn't sound happy.

Charlie went into the office. Craig watched her as she picked up the phone on his desk, then he turned his attention to a small stack of paperwork. Charlie said, "Hello?"

"Charlie, it's Memo! You need to come home right now!"

Charlie didn't want to appear alarmed in front of Craig. Trying to sound calm, she said, "What are you talking about?"

"Your house," Memo said over the phone. "It's... *alive*."

Chapter 11

Memo was standing on the lawn in front of Charlie's house, waiting for her, when she returned on her moped. The moped's tires screeched as she brought it to a stop. She jumped off, letting it fall to the ground.

"It's bad," Memo said. "It's really, really bad."

They ran to the front door, and Charlie shoved it open. Food and water were scattered across the living room floor, along with broken china and splintered wood. Deep scratches lined the walls. And then Charlie and Memo noticed the washer, which had grown stumpy metal legs and was walking in circles, leaking soapy water onto a rug.

But the washer wasn't the only appliance walking around. The refrigerator, dishwasher, and console television were also on the loose, lumbering around the house and breaking things. And the appliances had grown more than legs. They had bizarre combinations of arms, legs, eyes, and mouths.

The dishwasher made a gagging noise as it started throwing dinner plates across the living room. One plate smashed into Otis's video game console, shattering it. Charlie and Memo ducked, barely avoiding two plates that wound up crashing into the wall behind them. The dishwasher whipped another plate at Charlie, which smacked her in the forehead.

"Ouch!" she shouted. "Where's Bumblebee?"

Bumblebee's yellow head popped up from behind the kitchen counter. He looked sheepish and ashamed. Charlie ducked again as a coffee mug whizzed past her head. She said, "Bee! What did you do? What were you thinking? I told you to stay in the garage!"

Bumblebee lowered his head and crumpled, changing back to Beetle form in the middle of the living room.

"Great," Charlie said. "Helpful shame spiral, Bee."

The refrigerator lurched across the floor on tiny feet and lunged for Memo, opening and shutting its freezer door like a set of jaws. Memo grabbed a pillow from the ruined sofa, shoved it into the freezer, and slammed its door, trying to jam it up. The refrigerator paused, then made a gurgling noise followed by a loud burp. The refrigerator's door popped open, and pillow feathers flew out.

The refrigerator also contained a very anxious Conan. The dog jumped free of the refrigerator and ran around to hide behind the Beetle. Memo looked at the menacing appliances and said, "What *are* these things?" Suddenly, something on his left jerked into motion, and he turned to see the refrigerator coming at him again, its freezer door snapping at his head.

But just before the refrigerator could reach Memo, it shuddered and stopped, and then its feet retracted and vanished into its metal frame. Memo stared at what appeared to be an ordinary refrigerator. Charlie popped up from behind it, clutching a pair of pliers and a handful of wires and circuit boards that she'd yanked from the refrigerator's electrical system. The circuit boards were still glowing with green energy. She tossed the fried bits to the floor and shrugged, and the green energy fizzled before fading out. Then she saw the console television move across the living room, walking on a pair of long legs.

As Charlie tried to tackle the television, the washing machine lunged at Memo. He jumped on top of it and clung to it as he tried to reach its wiring. The washer began to spin like a top, whipping around and around in a tight circle. Memo said, "I think I'm going to barf."

The television dodged Charlie and walked over to a large mirror that hung on the wall. As images from random TV shows and bursts of static flickered across the screen, the television appeared to be fascinated by its reflection. Charlie tried to grab the television again, but it sidestepped her before it returned to the mirror, admiring itself.

"You look fine, okay?" Charlie said. She sprang forward, grabbed the television, and slammed it into the wall. The television tried to shake her off, but she locked her pliers onto its power cable and tugged. The television released a noisy burst of static as she tore the power cable out, and then its legs retracted into the console's base, but before it was properly balanced on the floor. The television wobbled, crashed against the floor, and cracked its glass screen.

As Charlie rose from the busted television, she heard a high-pitched electronic shriek. She turned and saw her alarm clock, which had changed into something that looked like a miniature robot monster. The alarm clock shrieked again, and Charlie almost jumped out of her skin. She swung her pliers at the screaming creature, but it skittered away and under an armchair.

Memo managed to disable the washing machine with his bare hands and turned his attention to the dishwasher. The dishwasher's door was open, and it was still hurling dinnerware all over the place. Memo dodged a thrown plate, weaved around the dishwasher, and threw himself headfirst into the open machine. The dishwasher thrashed back and forth, trying to eject Memo as he pulled away a filter and tried to reach the wiring.

Charlie darted over to a closet, opened it, and pulled out a baseball bat. Gripping the bat with one hand, she went to the armchair the alarm clock creature was using for a hiding place. "I've wanted to do this a long time," she said. She looked under the armchair. The creature was gone.

But then its earsplitting shriek came from behind her. Charlie spun and saw the alarm clock jumping up and down. She swung her bat at it but missed, smashing a vase instead. The alarm clock blared a mocking chitter as it ran off again.

Memo's head and upper body were still lodged inside the dishwasher as it tried to shake him loose. Just as he reached the machine's wiring, the dishwasher started to compress its frame in an effort to crush the human intruder. The machine's metal casing pressed against Memo as he tore out its circuitry. The dishwasher reverted to normal and went still. Memo pushed himself out of it and heard Charlie yell, "Shut up!"

She was yelling at the alarm clock and had resumed swinging her baseball bat at it. The alarm clock moved behind the sofa and made demented chirping and shrieking noises as it popped up and down, taunting Charlie. Charlie swung hard, and the bat connected, sending the alarm clock flying across the room and into a wall. The broken alarm clock fell to the floor, landed amid bits of broken dishes, and went silent.

Charlie and Memo looked at each other, and then they looked around. The house was a disaster. Bumblebee, still in Beetle form, remained parked in the living room. But the battle was over.

Looking again at Memo, Charlie said, "You okay?"

"I think so."

Charlie walked over to the Beetle. She placed her hand on the hood and said, "Bee, you've got to get out of here. I'm not mad. This is my fault. I never should have left you."

The Beetle's plating and other parts shifted as Bumblebee started to change into robot form, but Charlie said, "Maybe don't change all the way? We've got to get you back through the door."

Bumblebee tried to keep his body low and his arms close to his sides as Memo and Charlie guided him toward the ruined doorway to the garage. He managed to make it through, but because of his size and weight, he couldn't help inflicting more damage to the floor and woodwork. Once he had returned to the garage, Charlie looked back at the shambles of her house and said, "I'm in so much trouble."

But in the back of her mind, she had to wonder: If Bumblebee could cause this much damage by accident, what would intentional damage look like?

Sally picked up Otis at the karate dojo and drove straight home. She parked in their driveway, and they both got out. Otis was sucking on a lollipop as he said, "Hey, Mom, let me show you what I learned today."

"Sure, show me."

"Hi-yah!" Otis said before he moved around her, jumping and kicking and swinging at the air. One swing whizzed close to the back of Sally's head. "Hi-yah! And now you're crippled for life."

"Neat, honey," Sally said. "Watch the hair."

Inside the house, Charlie heard Sally's voice and looked at Memo. She and Memo had tried to reestablish order by pushing the broken appliances back into place, but the kitchen and living room still looked like disaster zones.

"Get out of here!" Charlie said to Memo. Memo scrambled toward the garage. Charlie ran fast for the front door, hoping to intercept her mother. "Mom, wait—!"

She was too late. The door swung open. Sally saw the ruined walls, floors, and furniture, and also the broken dishes. Then she looked at Charlie, and her face dropped.

Otis walked in behind Sally. He saw the wreckage, and the lollipop fell out of his mouth.

Sally said, "Oh my—"

"Okay," Charlie said. "Hold on a sec."

"Charlie, what the—?"

Otis shouted, "What'd you do to my TV?!" He stepped over and around the debris to inspect the console television. He looked queasy as he stared at its cracked screen. Then he noticed the remains of his video game system. He turned and fixed his gaze on Charlie. "You *monster.*"

Charlie looked from Otis to her mother. "You guys—"

Sally snapped and said, "What happened in here, Charlie?!"

Otis said, "You better ground her for literal life, Mom."

Charlie was thinking about how she could answer her mother's question when she looked through the broken doorway and into the garage. She saw Bumblebee changing back to car form as Memo gestured for her to come to them.

"Mom, I'll explain later," Charlie said. "I can't right now. I have to go."

"Are you kidding me?" Sally said. "You're not going anywhere!"

Charlie gestured to the doorway to the garage. "It's about my car, and it's really important."

"About your car?" Sally shook her head. "No, no, no. I've had it with this. You spend all day and night shut in that garage with that car!"

"Mom, I really can't—"

"No, you really *can*, Charlie. I've had enough."

Sally's face had turned red. "Your attitude, the constant sulking around, bringing home that wreck without even asking me. Everybody in this house is trying to be happy, and all you want to do is make things harder."

Charlie felt her chin trembling. Trying to sound calm, she said, "I'm so glad you and Ron and Otis are so happy, all three of you, with your new life together. But I can't just put on a smile and pretend Dad didn't die. I still miss him. I still hurt. But you don't care about me or how I'm feeling. The only time it matters to you is when it's ruining your good time. Well, sorry for bringing down your mood, Mom, but don't worry. In ten months, none of us will ever have to deal with each other."

Charlie turned and stormed off, heading to the garage. Sally yelled, "Charlie!"

Memo was in the Beetle. Charlie jumped in behind the wheel and said, "Go."

Bumblebee drove out of the garage and peeled off, carrying Charlie and Memo away from the cul-de-sac. Charlie was silent as Bumblebee steered onto a winding road. Memo looked at her and said, "You okay?"

Charlie thought, *Nope*. But she said, "Yep."

"Look," Memo said, "if you don't want to talk about it, I understand. But you seem pretty upset, so..."

Charlie gazed at the road ahead and considered whether she wanted to tell Memo why she was upset. When she finally spoke, her voice was quiet. "I just feel like ever since my dad died, I've become this drain on everyone, and I hate it...." She looked out the side window as she tried to sort out words to describe her feelings. "Trust me, I want to move on and feel better...it's just...his stuff is every-where in that house, all around me. And I can't handle looking at it. But I can't handle *not* looking at it, either...." She returned her gaze to the road in front of Bumblebee. "Everything will be better when I can just leave and go someplace to start over."

Memo looked through the front window, too. "I didn't know your dad passed away. I'm really sorry."

Charlie glanced at Memo. She sensed his sincerity and appreciated his condolences, but words caught in her throat. She didn't know what to say.

Memo said, "There's this quote for hard times.... I'm not a big 'quote' guy, but I've always liked it."

Charlie waited for him to continue. "Yeah?"

"*'The darkest nights produce the brightest stars.'*"

Charlie smiled. "That's nice."

Memo smiled back. "My mom got it from Weight Watchers."

As the Beetle drove on along the country road, Charlie began to worry about Bumblebee. She still had many questions about him, his origins, and his connection with the hologram in the woods. And what about the Decepticons? Were they a threat to humans? More than anything, she worried about her ability to take care of Bumblebee. She could only imagine what the future would bring, but she vowed to stick close to Bumblebee no matter what.

Epilogue

In a secret underground base, Agent Burns watched the two large, menacing robots named Shatter and Dropkick as they studied a computer screen that displayed a map of North America's southwest coast. The screen also displayed data gathered from a makeshift information network. Now that more Cybertronians had come to Earth, Burns had made a reluctant alliance, desperate to find the robot he had failed to capture.

Shatter noticed a tiny area of the map go dark, and then a utility company's report appeared in a separate window on the screen. Shatter studied the data. "Brighton Falls power company just reported a back surge at 437.6 megahertz."

"We found him!" Dropkick said. "We found B-127!"

Dropkick and Shatter turned to face Agent Burns. Burns's eyes narrowed on the map as he plotted the route for Brighton Falls. "We're coming for you, B-127," Burns said, "and we're coming right now." The robots exchanged a glance—their plan was finally coming to fruition.

Burns gave orders to the soldiers under his command, and they boarded their fleet of armed and armored vehicles. As Shatter and Dropkick exited the underground base with the fleet, their body parts began to slide and reconfigure until both robots had changed into a pair of souped-up Baja racers. They roared off, leaving a high trail of dust.

They were very eager to see B-127 again.